"Are You Trying To Get Rid Of Me, Tess?" Damien Asked.

"My partners are on their way over here and they know—"

"Nothing about me?" Damien finished for her, a flash of venomous pleasure lighting his eyes.

"They know nothing about my life before we started the company."

He considered this for a moment, then nodded. "All right. I'll see you tomorrow, Tess."

She looked up. "What?"

"I'll be at your office tomorrow at one."

"No!"

Damien leaned in close to Tess's ear, the heat from his breath making her hair stand on end and her heart twist painfully. This she remembered, and long ago, this she had loved.

"I'm not here to reminisce about old times," he uttered darkly. "I'm here to collect on a debt that was never paid."

Dear Reader,

I don't want it to end.

LOL…

Seriously, I loved writing this series. Three strong women with secrets who run a wife-for-hire agency out of my hometown of Minneapolis…then slide three incredibly hot, alpha males in there to torment them.

LOVE IT!

Rich Man's Vengeful Seduction was the first book I thought of for this series. I wanted a hero who was as close to a devil as I could get. A millionaire bad boy who was just as wounded as the heroine and would believe he had to make her suffer as much as she'd unknowingly made him suffer. And I came up with Damien Sauer. I think the concept of two people who have known each other before, have loved, have been intimate, then one leaves, is an incredibly powerful plotline and my absolute favorite to write.

I hope you enjoy! Shoot me an e-mail and let me know what you think.

laura@laurawright.com

Best,

Laura

LAURA WRIGHT

RICH MAN'S VENGEFUL SEDUCTION

Silhouette®

Desire

Published by Silhouette Books

America's Publisher of Contemporary Romance

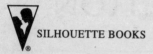

SILHOUETTE BOOKS

ISBN-13: 978-0-373-76839-4
ISBN-10:   0-373-76839-7

RICH MAN'S VENGEFUL SEDUCTION

Recent books by Laura Wright

Silhouette Desire

Redwolf's Woman #1582
A Bed of Sand #1607
The Sultan's Bed #1661
Her Royal Bed #1674
Savor the Seduction #1687
*Millionaire's Calculated Baby Bid #1828
*Playboy's Ruthless Payback #1834
*Rich Man's Vengeful Seduction #1839

*No Ring Required

LAURA WRIGHT

has spent most of her life immersed in the world of acting, singing and competitive ballroom dancing. But when she started writing romance, she knew she'd found her true calling! Born and raised in Minneapolis, Laura has also lived in New York City, Milwaukee and Columbus, Ohio. Currently, she is happy to have set down her bags and made Los Angeles her home. And a blissful home it is—one that she shares with her theatrical production manager husband, Daniel, and three spoiled dogs. During those few hours of downtime from her beloved writing, Laura enjoys going to art galleries and movies, cooking for her hubby, walking in the woods, lazing around lakes, puttering in the kitchen and frolicking with her animals. Laura would love to hear from you. You can write to her at P.O. Box 5811 Sherman Oaks, CA 91413 or e-mail her at laura@laurawright.com.

To Isa, the strongest, smartest
and most amazing four-year-old I know!

One

There was nothing more unsettling than a devil in church.

Swathed in a black chiffon Vera Wang bridesmaid dress, her red hair piled on top of her head, Tess York stared at the man in the fourth pew, her palms going damp around the base of her bouquet of red peonies. His name was Damien Sauer and he was tall, dark and fierce looking—just as she remembered him. Once upon a time they had been together, boyfriend and girlfriend, lovers and friends, but then another man had come along. A man who was mild and shy and had seemed the safe choice at the time. Back then, she'd been a sucker for safe, and had walked away from Damien and the look of seething animosity that had followed her out the door.

The scent of pine from the decorative holiday garland strewn around the church ceased being romantic and festive and instead gave way to a horrible bout of nausea. *What is he doing back here?* she wondered nervously. He didn't belong here anymore. As far as she knew, he'd gotten out of Minnesota years ago and had moved to California. Rumor had it that he'd taken on the real estate market, flipping houses at the rate of two per month. Supposedly, he was unstoppable, went into every deal without a conscience and was now worth millions.

Tess was hardly surprised by his success. Six years ago he'd worked as lead carpenter for a construction company in town. His ideas were so clever, so innovative, his handiwork so skillful and beautiful, he was wanted by every contractor in the city.

But local jobs and local pay hadn't been enough for Damien. He'd wanted more and had been willing to risk everything to get where he wanted to go.

Tess watched him sit immobile in his seat with that arrogant lift to his chin as he witnessed Mary and Ethan exchange wedding vows. Tension moved through her neck and shoulders like a snake in search of a fat mouse. She had done everything to bury her wretched, mistake-filled past, erase the so-called life she'd lived, married to the most worthless of husbands. Along with her partners, Olivia Winston and Mary Kelley, she'd helped build a winning wife-for-hire business and had created a smooth, comfortable life for herself. All she wanted to do these days was act as though the past had never existed and continue to live happily and cautiously in the present.

But the devil had shown up in church.

Behind her, someone took to the keys of the piano, playing the introduction to *Phantom's* "All I Ask of You." Everyone in the wedding party turned—as rehearsed—to watch the two performers walk to the piano, then sing.

Everyone except Tess.

She couldn't take her eyes off Damien. Maybe if she stared hard enough at him he'd get up and leave. She almost laughed out loud at the stupid thought. He wasn't a man to be chased out, scared off. He had the strongest will of anyone she had ever known.

Her gaze moved over him. He had grown leaner in the body and broader in the shoulders since she'd last seen him, but his mouth was as hard as his expression now, as though he didn't make a habit of smiling.

What is he here for? Does he know Ethan? Or God forbid, Mary?

Tess shifted, her black heels feeling suffocatingly tight. There was no way she was ready to spill her guts about the past to her partners…

Beside her, No Ring Required's culinary expert, Olivia Winston leaned in. "Hey, I know the singing's not Broadway caliber, but no spacing out, okay?"

"Yeah. Right. Sure," Tess muttered, utterly distracted.

The pretty brunette frowned at her. "What's wrong with you?"

"Nothing," Tess said quickly.

"Doesn't look like nothing," Olivia muttered.

Refusing to make a scene at her partner's wedding, Tess forced herself to face the singers. She had to get a grip here. Maybe Damien didn't even know she was there—maybe he'd forgotten all about her. Maybe he was married…with two kids and a dog named Buster. After all it had been six years. Look at all that had happened to her….

But as she half listened to the singers belt it out for the bride and groom, the music swelling and filling the church, she had an odd feeling, as though she were being watched, as though little bugs were crawling into the red curls at her hairline and nipping at her skin. It was a feeling she'd had only one time before.

The day she'd turned her back on the devilish Damien Sauer and walked out.

"Sir, would you like me to take you home?"

As his driver navigated through the congested downtown Minneapolis traffic, Damien sat in the back of his limousine, the collar of his black coat kissing the hard line of his jaw. "No. I'm going to the Georgian."

"I'm sorry sir. I don't think I heard you—"

"Take me to the Georgian Hotel," Damien said evenly. "I'm going to the reception."

"But, sir, you never go…" The driver's voice trailed off.

"Is there a problem, Robert?" Damien asked impatiently, as outside the long, black car, snowflakes pelted the windows.

"Sir?" Robert glanced up into the rearview mirror, his pale brown eyes not exactly meeting that of his employer's. "If I can speak frankly—"

Damien raised a brow. "You may...if you keep your eyes on the road while doing it. This isn't the dry and mild Los Angeles weather. The roads in Minneapolis can be pretty slick."

"Yes, sir." Robert turned his attention back to the road, two hands locked to the wheel.

Damien released a breath. "So, what do you want to know?"

"In the four years I have been working for you, this is the first wedding reception of a business associate you have ever attended."

"Is it?" Damien said tonelessly.

"Yes, sir."

"Hmm."

"Very important business then, sir?"

The car slowed, made a turn then stopped. Damien looked up, frowned. "Are we here?"

"Yes, sir, but there's a line of cars ahead of us."

They were more than a few yards from the entrance to the hotel, but Damien wasn't a man to wait. He reached for the door handle and pulled. "I'll get out here, Robert."

"But, sir?" The driver glanced over his shoulder, uncertain. "Shall I—"

"No, no. Stay in the car."

Robert nodded. "All right, sir."

Damien was half out the door when he turned back. "And, Robert?"

"Yes, sir."

"To answer your question, this reception is about something far more important than business." He stepped out of the car. "Be out front in one hour."

The ballroom in the Georgian Hotel was *the* most spectacular sight in Minneapolis for a wedding reception, beautifully appointed with gilded ceilings, crystal chandeliers and a black-and-white-marble dance floor. In any season the room could knock you off your feet, but in December, there was an extra shot of fabulous as the ballroom was decked out in white Christmas lights, spruce trees, mistletoe, and atop every black glass place setting, handmade chocolate candy canes nestled sweetly inside mini Christmas stockings.

Tess York was a self-described chocoholic, and five minutes after her arrival to the hotel her mini stocking was empty. Beside her seat was Olivia's, and the only reason a candy cane still lay safely on her plate was that Tom Radley, No Ring Required's very first client five years ago, and a family friend of Mary's, had taken Tess by the hand and forced her onto the dance floor before she could snatch it up.

On a rectangular stage beside the dance floor, a woman who sounded shockingly similar to Natalie Cole belted out love songs.

Next to Tess, Olivia and her fiancé, Mac Valentine, moved to the music. The pair were so handsome, so sharp looking they could have easily been mistaken for a Hollywood couple. Stunning in a black bridesmaid dress similar to Tess's, her dark hair long and loose about her bare shoulders, Olivia turned her brown doe eyes on Tess and cracked a smile. "You are one amazingly bad dancer, you know that?"

"Gee, thanks," Tess said dryly.

"Not true," insisted Tom Radley, sidestepping to avoid contact with the heel of Tess's shoe as she executed an awkward spin. "Don't listen to her, Tess." He glared at Olivia. "She's as graceful as a swan, light as a feather."

Olivia snorted. "As long as she doesn't step on your feet, right?"

"Easy now, my love," Mac said, pulling his girl closer.

Tess made a gesture with her hand as though she was flicking away an annoying bug. "Move along, Winston. I'm sure there are other people on this dance floor whose self-esteem you can destroy tonight."

Olivia laughed. "Right. As if you could ever be bested, Tess. You have more confidence in your little pinky than a grizzly bear at feeding time."

"Hmm," Tess said, her brow creased. "Not sure how I should take that."

Ever the gentleman, Mac jumped in. "As a compliment. And I think you dance beautifully." He attempted to look innocent, but the guy's smile had way too much rascal in it to be believable.

"Flattery won't get you anywhere with me, Mr. Valentine," Tess said, ducking her head to walk underneath Tom's arm as he led her into a spin.

Mac shrugged, then turned to his fiancé and leaned in to kiss her neck. "How about you? Will flattery get me anywhere with you?"

Olivia snuggled closer in his arms. "Yup."

Tess rolled her eyes. Leaning into her partner, she whispered, "Let's move away from the lovebirds before the cherubs flying over their heads accidentally shoot us with their arrows."

Laughing, Tom said, "You got it," and steered her away.

But when they reached the other side of the dance floor, there was a man standing there. He was clearly waiting for them, his cool blue eyes regarding them with an interested, though unfriendly stare. He was tall, wide in the shoulders and dressed in a very expensive tux. His black hair was cropped short and his full mouth looked hard and capable of cruel words.

Tess's heart leaped into her throat and remained there, pounding away unsympathetically. It was one thing to have him sitting ten feet away, his gaze trained on Mary and Ethan as they gave themselves to each other—it was another to have him in front of her, reaching for her hand.

Damien Sauer glanced at Tom, lifted an eyebrow. "If you don't mind."

Slightly nervous, Tom's answer came out sounding winded. "Of course I mind. But…well, I'm good at sharing."

"That's admirable," Damien said darkly, easing Tess from Tom's arms into his own. "I'm not."

Tess was not the kind of woman who would allow a man to call the shots—not anymore, at any rate. If anyone else at any other time had jumped in and pulled her away from her partner the way Damien had, she'd have been tempted to deck him. But this man was different, and so was her reaction to him. It was as though time had never separated them, and once in his arms, she felt so good, so warm, she didn't even attempt to pull away from him.

As the music played all around them, Damien settled into a slow rhythm, his gaze burning into hers. "Hello, Tess."

She hadn't said his name out loud in six years. Guess now was as good a time as any. "Damien Sauer. Wow. It's been a long time."

"Not that long," he said. His voice was deep, deeper than she remembered, but the tone was the same and it washed over her, bringing back a hundred different emotions. "I saw you at the engagement party, and I thought you saw me. Maybe not."

"No, I did. I mean, yes. But I didn't think…" She shrugged at her own inability to speak coherently. "I guess I wasn't sure…"

"You're stuttering, Tess," he said, arching a brow. "That's not like you."

No, it wasn't. But strange, complicated things had always happened when this man touched her. And right now his hand, wrapped lightly around hers, and his body just inches away were making her breathe a little funny. "What I was trying to say, completely inarticulately, was that I didn't know you and Ethan were friends."

"We're not," he said plainly. "He's looking to buy one of my properties and I was looking for an invitation to his wedding."

Her heart dropped. "Really?"

"Yes."

"Why?"

He gave her a sardonic grin. "I've heard that your business is quite a success," he said, ignoring her question. "You've done well for yourself."

His words sounded more like an observation than a compliment. "I think so. But not as well as you, it seems."

He nodded. "After you left town, I became very focused."

Of course he was going to go there. Make her damn uncomfortable, maybe break out in a sweat. "Well, focused can be good."

"Yes, it can. In fact, I might go so far as to say that I owe a great deal of my fortune to you."

The scent of the spruce tree to their left was overpowering. "I'm sure that's not—"

"Don't be so modest, Tess. You were an inspiration…"

It was too much. The whole thing—his sardonic compliments, her nervousness. She was not going to put herself in the position of being freaked out around a man anymore. She stopped dancing. Music played and people swayed, but she stared expectantly at Damien Sauer. "What's going on here? Why did you come?"

"I wanted to see you." There was zero warmth behind his eyes, and the look he gave her chilled the blood in her veins.

"Well, you saw me," she said, turning away. "Thank you for the dance."

He took her hand and placed it through his arm. "I'll take you back to your table."

She thought about wrenching her arm free, but she wasn't going to cause a scene, so she let him lead her. As they walked, Tess couldn't help but notice the way women stared at Damien: hungry, needy. Just the way she'd stared at him once upon a time.

When they got to the table reserved for the wedding party, Tess sat and hoped that Damien would just take off, that the dance and the verbal sparring would be the end of it. But he didn't leave. Instead he sat beside her.

"So, how's Henry?" His voice was low and cold.

She stared at him, looked into those deep blue eyes and found clarity. He wasn't here on business or to just "see" her. He'd come to the wedding to confront her or hurt her. But why now, after six years, she wasn't sure. She looked directly into his eyes and said evenly, "My husband passed away. About five years ago."

Damien nodded, but didn't look surprised. "I'm sorry."

"Are you?"

His brows lifted. "I could say no but what would that make me?"

She shrugged. "Cruel."

"How about honest?"

"How about both?"

Out of the corner of her eye, Tess spotted Mary and Olivia on the other side of the dance floor, and her heart jumped. They were staring at her and Damien, curious looks on their faces. Tess knew her partners well enough to know that in about thirty seconds they were going to be headed her way. She wasn't about to have her past and past mistakes laid bare at her partner's wedding.

She turned back to Damien, hoping that her face had not gone pale. "Dinner is going to be served soon. Maybe we can catch up another time."

"Are you trying to get rid of me, Tess?" he asked, studying her face.

"No."

"I can tell when you're lying. Always could."

"Fine." Her jaw tightened. "My partners are on their way over here and they know—"

"Nothing about me?" Damien finished for her, a flash of venomous pleasure lighting his eyes.

"They know nothing about you or Henry or my life before we started the company."

"Why is that?"

"It's none of your business." There was no time for this. Mary and Olivia were just a few feet away. "You can say whatever you need to say. But not here, not now. Another time."

He considered this for a moment, then nodded. "All right."

Relief accosted her, and she said quickly, "Okay. Goodbye, then."

He stood. "I'll see you tomorrow, Tess."

She looked up. "What?"

"I'll be at your office tomorrow at one."

"No!"

Mary and Olivia were almost upon them. Damien leaned in close to Tess's ear, the heat from his breath making her hair stand on end and her heart twist painfully. This she remembered, and long ago this she had loved.

"I'm not here to reminisce about old times," he uttered darkly. "I'm here to collect on a debt that was never paid."

Tess's head started spinning. What debt was he talking about?

"Six years ago," he continued, "you made a promise to me. One that was never fulfilled. I'm here to make sure you fulfill it. Because if you don't, everything you hold dear will crumble."

He stood just in time to greet Mary and Olivia, shaking their hands and complimenting the bride on the ceremony and reception. Dumbstruck, Tess just stared at her plate and the empty stocking. Through the din of her overactive brain, she heard Damien wish them both well, then walk away.

"Nice," Olivia said, taking her seat beside Tess. "Very cute."

"Gorgeous and charming," Mary remarked, righting her tiara before sitting in the chair designated for the bride. "And looking smitten with our girl here."

"Did you get his number, Tess?" Olivia asked.

Tess nodded and said hoarsely, "Yes. I've got his number all right."

Two

In the four and a half years that Tess York had been with No Ring Required, she'd called in sick three times. The first time was in the winter of 2004, when she'd had the flu so badly, she'd passed out on the way to her car. The second time was last summer when she'd had her wisdom teeth out, and the third time was today when she'd woken up with a nasty little hangover.

She wasn't a big drinker. Actually she wasn't even a little drinker, but last night, after seeing Damien and having the past hurled back in her face, she'd enjoyed a few glasses of champagne too many.

Garbed in ratty old sweats and stretched out on the couch with her cat, Hepburn, Tess stared at the TV. Trying to ignore her pounding head, she watched

Montel Williams take a seat beside his favorite psychic guest, who was telling one audience member after another that what they probably had in their house was a ghost who had unfinished business.

"Maybe you can give us some advice on how to get rid of those ghosts," Tess muttered at the screen.

So far, she'd only taken steps to avoid hers. Mary was already on her honeymoon, so Olivia was going to be the only one in to work today. The one appointment Tess did have wasn't on the books, and she was more than willing to skip it.

As the psychic rambled on about heaven and the light, Tess let her eyes close and her mind shut off for a while. She must've drifted off because when she woke up, there was a soap opera on the television and someone knocking on her apartment door. Her head still pounding, she padded over to the door and looked out the peephole.

When she saw who it was, she swore silently, turned around and sagged against the door.

Damien.

"Tess?"

Accompanying her headache, her stomach twisted sickly at the sound of his voice.

"Tess, I know you're there."

"What do you want, Damien?" she yelled into the door.

"You know exactly what I want. I was pretty damn clear last night. Now open the door."

"I'm sick."

"Yes, Olivia was kind enough to tell me that. After I'd driven all the way over there."

Tess sighed. This was not how she did things—hiding behind doors so she wouldn't have to deal with uncomfortable meetings and threats from an old boyfriend. That was the way the married Tess had handled herself, the Tess who'd had a reason to feel nervous and afraid. But that part of her life was over.

She flipped the lock and opened the door wide.

Damien stood there, filling up her doorway. Freshly shaven and showered and dressed in a navy blue suit so fine it probably came straight from the Gucci runway show in Milan.

Knowing she looked like her cat's chew toy after a gnarly play session, she lifted her chin and said in her most superior tone, "I never agreed to see you, Damien."

A slow, cool smile curved his lips as he looked her over. "Well, there she is."

"There who is?"

"The firecracker I used to know. The woman worthy of that mass of red hair." He leaned against the doorjamb. "After last night and hearing all that stuttering and fear of what your partners might find out, I thought she was gone. I wondered what or who had taken that fire out of her."

Well, he could keep on wondering, she thought dryly. There was no way he was ever going to know anything about her life with Henry, about the scars that remained.

He narrowed his eyes, studied her. "You look…"

"Sick?" she offered.

"Did you drink last night?"

"That's really none of your business."

"Champagne gives you intense headaches, remember?"

"No," she lied.

He crossed his arms over his chest. "Are you going to let me in?"

"I think you can say whatever cryptic thing you need to say from here."

"Fine, but I did bring you matzo ball soup…well, actually Robert picked it up." He held up a white deli bag. "And you look like you could use it. But you can't eat it standing in the entryway."

"Who's Robert?"

"My driver?"

She rolled her eyes. "There's a point at which someone has too much money."

"Not really."

He tried to walk past her, but she stopped him. "Soup first."

He handed her the bag, and she let him pass. After a quick look around her living room, he sat on the couch. She picked up the remote and switched off the television, then dropped into the leather armchair a few feet away.

His brow lifted. "Are you afraid of me?"

"Fear is a useless emotion," she began. But then she shrugged. Instead of inspirational quotes, maybe honesty…or some form of hybrid might be a better tack to take with this man. "After what you said last night, or didn't say, I think feeling apprehensive isn't a bizarre response."

His gaze grew serious, his mouth hard. "No."

She placed the deli bag on the coffee table, then looked up at him. "Enough bantering back and forth. You and I both know this isn't a social call, so let's get to it."

He sat back and regarded her. "Do you remember the red house in Tribute?"

A rush of memories flooded into her mind along with a deep burn of sadness. It had been their spot, a starter home, in a tiny town, that Damien had bought for a song as his first investment property. In the high days of their romance, they had walked the main drag of that town, sharing their plans for the future, then later they'd shared a bed.

She met his gaze and nodded. "I remember."

"I want to renovate it."

This surprised her. "You never did?"

"No."

"Okay. So, what does this have to do with me?"

"You made a promise to me in that house, one week before you left."

Tess's heart plummeted into her stomach, and she searched her memory.

"You promised to help me renovate. You wanted to make it a home, if I recall correctly." His voice dropped, soured. "I expect you to keep that promise."

"You can't be serious?"

"I am."

And then it all came back in a rush. It had happened a week before she left, just like he'd said. One week before Henry had asked her to be his wife. One week before she'd forced herself to realize that with a man like Damien she'd never have the kind of life she'd planned for herself. The kind of stable, family-friendly life she'd promised herself when she was seventeen, after her parents' deaths. She stared at him and shook her head. "But why? Why do you care now—"

"It's a chapter I need to finish," he said, his tone cool. He stood, then reached inside his coat and pulled out an envelope. "Here are the keys, the address—in case you've forgotten—and a formidable amount of cash."

"What—"

"I need you to start right away."

He was crazy. She stood. "Damien, I have no intention of—"

"I need the job done in two weeks."

She didn't even try to suppress a bitter laugh. "Impossible."

"I leave in two weeks, back to California. I want to make sure everything is done. And I want a full remodel, not just a coat of paint and new towels for the bathroom."

She put up a hand. "Stop right now. This is not going to happen. Two weeks is Christmas."

He shrugged. "You can do your shopping up in Tribute."

"Not funny, Damien. I have a business to run—"

"Yes, and if it will make you feel better, tell your partners that I hired you." His gaze moved over her hungrily. "My wife for hire for two weeks, fixing up my home."

Awareness moved through her, but she shook it off. She walked to the apartment door and opened it. "I'm not going to play this game with you anymore."

He didn't move. "Good, because I don't play games. You will go to Tribute and you will fix up the house."

"Or what?"

"Or that business of yours will have to find a new location, which will take a lot of time and money that a new business can't really afford."

"Are you actually threatening me?" The words ground out from between her teeth. "Because I don't take kindly to threats."

"I'm telling you to think about your future," he said, his tone dark with warning. "And the future of your partners."

"What the hell does that mean?"

He walked to her, faced her. "I know the owner of your building and I think I could convince him to not renew your lease in January."

Her heart took a nosedive. "How do you know our lease is up in January?" She was shaking now, her breathing uneven. "Do you have this jerk owner in your pocket?"

"I don't have to. I'm the jerk."

Tess held her breath, and silence filled the space. She was trying to process what he had said and, more important, what it meant.

"I own your building, Tess."

She shook her head. "I don't believe you."

"My company owns your building," he said evenly. "Three years now."

"Why are you doing this?"

"I have a business, too."

"What is this business of yours? Revenge? Hurt feelings because I chose another man over you?"

He seemed to grow a foot taller before her eyes, and his gaze became dark and menacing.

She looked directly at him. "You need to grow up, Damien."

His lips formed a sneer. "I'll expect you at the house tomorrow afternoon. Don't disappoint me."

"Who are you?" she called after him as he walked down the hall. "The man I used to know would never do something like—"

"The *boy* you used to know was a fool," he said over his shoulder as he walked into the elevator. "Enjoy the soup."

Tess shut the door with a little too much force. That bastard. *Never. No way.* He could take his threats and shove them where the sun don't shine. She spotted the deli bag on the coffee table and snatched it up, stalked into the kitchen. But as she dumped the soup into the sink, her rational mind started to rear its unwanted head. If he did own her building—a fact she would check immediately—he could follow through on his threat and kick them all out on their backsides.

Did he really hate her that much…?

Tess leaned on the counter and released a breath. Her headache from earlier was gone, but it looked like she was about to get another…one that would last about two weeks.

According to some major athletes and those perfect people who work out a lot, exercise is the best way of reaching a state of true introspection.

Well, Tess was counting on it.

"So, renovating a house? Like new paint and drywall? Or we talking air ducts and toilet flanges?"

It was 7:00 a.m. and Tess had met Olivia at the gym for a workout. Earlier that morning, say around 6:15, she'd sat in her office at NRR and gone over lease agreement after lease agreement, only to discover that Damien's company did indeed own her building. It hadn't taken her long to get it—there was nothing to do but face the fire. Damien was in need of some vengeance, and from the look on his face yesterday he wasn't going to hesitate to kick them all out of the building if Tess didn't comply with his demands.

So, at eleven o'clock, she was leaving for Tribute. She'd get in, do the job and get out.

"I'm not sure what I'll find when I get there," Tess said to Olivia, her breathing uneven as she picked up the pace when the treadmill inclined a notch. "Guess I'll have to wait and see."

Beside Tess, Olivia rode a stationary bike at a snail's pace. "The client didn't give you specifics?"

"He asked for a full remodel."

"Who is the client, by the way? Do I know him?"

Tess hesitated. She wanted to tread lightly here. "He's the man from Mary and Ethan's wedding."

Olivia's brows shot up. "Mr. Tall, Dark and Dreamy? The one who came into NRR looking for you yesterday?"

"That's the one."

"Wow. He moves pretty fast."

Tess bit her lip. She hated to lie to her partner, but there was no way she was going to explain the past and the present circumstances. Or what was at stake if she didn't take this job. "We spoke this morning. He needs the job done ASAP. He needs to get back to California in a couple weeks."

"He's looking to sell the place?"

"I think so."

"That's a big job to take on right before Christmas. You sure you want to tackle it?"

"Yeah. Not a problem. I'll probably do a good portion of the work myself, then hire a few subcontractors."

"You're gonna have to pay double because of the holiday." Sweat-free and smiling, Olivia stepped off the bike and came to stand by the treadmill. "Speaking of which, what are you doing for Christmas?"

Ah…same thing she did every year. Join a few people in her building on Christmas Eve for some food and music, then just relax on Christmas Day. She shrugged. "Not sure."

"I want you to spend the day with Mac and me."

Tess grinned at her partner. It was a nice offer. "That's sweet, Liv. But—"

"No buts."

Tess stepped off the treadmill and grabbed her towel. "We'll see."

"And you know," Olivia continued. "Mac has a friend…"

"That's nice," Tess said quickly. "Everyone needs friends."

Cocking her head to the side, Olivia gave her a soft smile. "I want you find the right man."

"I don't want the right man, Liv."

Olivia laughed. "How about the wrong one, then?"

Been there, done that. She tossed Olivia a tight smile. "I have to go home. Shower and change, take the cat to the vet, then get on the road."

She nodded. "I'll call you."

"Okay."

Tess owned a pretty great SUV. It was sleek and black, had four-wheel drive, leather seats, a killer sound system and an easily accessible cup holder for her coffee. It also had a panel that displayed the outside temperature.

Normally Tess glanced at this panel once during her regular drive time, but on this trip she'd checked the thing every few minutes. Mostly because she couldn't believe how quickly the temperature dropped—five degrees every thirty minutes.

Northern Minnesota in winter was as close to the Arctic as most people ever got. Freezing temperatures arrived in October and stayed around until April, making everyone up there a bit nutty. Tess shook her head. And she was about to spend the next two weeks there. Good thing she'd packed her parka.

Just before two o'clock, she pulled off the freeway and drove the short distance to downtown Tribute, which was comprised of four wide, unclogged streets with a handful of mom-and-pop stores, a gas station and a diner. It hadn't changed much in six years, and for a moment Tess recalled how she and Damien had shared a burger in the diner and a good deal of necking behind the gas station.

Tess slowed to a crawl as she drove down Yarr Lane, then pulled into the third driveway on the left. She killed the engine and stepped out of the car. The yard was three feet deep in snow, but other than that the little red cottage looked very much the same as it had. Which, incidentally wasn't saying much.

To start with it needed a fresh coat of paint, a

clean doorknob, coach lamp, knocker and new address numbers. And that was just on the outside.

As she walked to the door, she recalled thinking that Damien had bought this house for them, for a future together. But he had been quick to point out that he'd purchased the house as an investment property: the first of many—to be fixed up and sold for a profit. Hearing that had crushed her, made her realize that they'd wanted very different things from life.

She unlocked the house and stepped inside. It was completely bare, not one piece of furniture, and there was dust on every visible surface.

She did a quick walk through and found that the two small bedrooms were well maintained, just in need of a cleaning, new fixtures and a few coats of paint. The kitchen and bathroom, however, were, in a word, horrible. Outdated and showing years of wear. Both spaces needed new floors, countertops, some drywall patching, new appliances, fixtures and paint.

She stood in the living room and stared. The place needed a lot, a complete overhaul. First thing she had to do was go into town, get some cleaning supplies and the phone numbers of some skilled labor.

"So you're the city girl Damien hired?"

Startled, Tess whirled around. Walking into the house was a woman in her late sixties, bundled up in a dark-blue down jacket and matching ski cap. She had smooth chocolate-brown skin, high cheekbones and cat-shaped violet eyes. She was short and a little plump, but even at her age she was startlingly beautiful.

Tess stuck out a hand. "Hi, I'm Tess York."

"Wanda Bennett," the woman said, shaking Tess's hand with the firm grip of a lumberjack. "I'm the property manager here in Tribute, and the owner of the food market in town."

"It's nice to meet you."

The woman nodded, then glanced around. "Sweet place, but it needs some work."

"Sure does," Tess agreed.

"Never understood why Damien left it to rot like this. Not his style."

No, it wasn't his style. And he had just left the place to rot until he'd found the time to blackmail his former girlfriend into fixing it up. Tess didn't think that sharing this information with Wanda was appropriate. Of course, the woman had called Damien by his first name, so maybe they were friends, maybe she knew exactly who Tess was and what she was doing here.

"So, you're probably wondering why I barged in like this?" Wanda asked.

"You said you're the property manager…"

"Sure, I turned on the heat and water, but Damien wanted me to give you this." She took a fat envelope out of her jacket pocket and handed it to Tess. "Here."

"What is it?"

"He wired it this morning. He thought you might need more than what he gave you," Wanda explained.

"For fixing up the place. He wants it furnished, as well."

Tess looked inside the envelope. A three-inch stack of hundred-dollar bills. Good Lord. He'd already given her four times that much. But then again you never knew what problems might come up in an older house. She looked up at Wanda again. "Is there a furniture store in town?"

"Nope."

"Lighting, hardware?"

"There is a hardware store in Tribute—it's on Main, next to the diner—and you can get furniture and light fixtures in Jackson, that's about fifty miles away." She paused for a moment, then said, "But I think Damien might want this place fixed up with the local flavor. A few people make their own furnishings around here, I'd talk to them."

"Do they work quickly? I'm under a bit of a time crunch."

Wanda shrugged. "Depends."

Tess sighed. Looked as though she was just going to have to figure everything out on her own. She gave Wanda a quick smile and said, "I'm going to head over to the motel and check in, then."

"Ruby's place?"

"Yes. I saw it in the phone book."

Wanda pressed her lips together and looked at the ceiling.

"Is something wrong?"

"Nope."

Tess's shoulders fell. "What? Is Ruby an ax murder or something?"

"No. Ruby's lovely." She pointed to the envelope in Tess's hand. "It's just that before you go to Ruby's, you might want to go here first."

Tess glanced down at the address written on the envelope. "What is this?"

"Damien asked that you be there at four o'clock."

"Four o'clock when?"

"Today," Wanda said evenly.

Tess looked down at her watch. "It's three-thirty now."

She waved her hand as if it was nothing to worry about. "It's just a short drive. I'll give you directions."

On a sigh, Tess grabbed her purse and searched for a pen. She had really wanted to clean up the place before it got dark. Damn Damien and his demands. "So, what's at this address?" she asked Wanda. "A contractor or a plumber or something."

Wanda shrugged her shoulders again. "Or something."

Tess glared at her. "Did Damien tell you to be this annoyingly evasive?"

At that, a smile tugged at the woman's lips and she pointed to the pen in Tess's hand. "I'll give you those directions now."

Three

The drive took under five minutes, but it was all uphill, and the roads were slick, as daylight had decided to knock off a little early. When Tess pulled into the driveway and saw the house, she thought she'd made a mistake with the directions. She glanced down to check if she had the correct address.

She did.

Who in the world lived here? she wondered. An artist? A famous, reclusive artist who had cut off his ear, then moved to Tribute for the peace and quiet and frigid climate?

Tess got out of the car to a blast of arctic air and looked up at the massive glass fortress. Whoever lived here, she mused, had better have something to do with the renovating process.

She walked to the front door. It wouldn't surprise her if this was some kind of roadblock that Damien had put up to mess with her—picking out artwork for the walls before they were even painted, or something equally wasteful in the time management department. Sure, he wanted the house done in two weeks, but he wanted to make every move she made that much more difficult in the process.

Her teeth chattering, she rang the bell. Thankfully, she didn't have to wait more than ten seconds before it opened. For a moment she thought she'd come face-to-face with Danny Devito. Then she realized the impossibility of such a thought and granted the man a friendly smile. "Hello. I'm Tess York. I have an appointment."

"Of course." He stepped aside. "Please come in."

The first thing Tess noticed when she walked into the entryway was how warm the space was. Not the architecture. That was sleek and sexy and ultramodern. But warm in temperature. Even with the sun going down outside, the light that had been filtering in from the many windows all day heated the house toasty warm.

The man she'd mentally referred to as Danny Devito took her coat, then gestured toward the open living area. The space was perfectly outfitted with expensive, modern furnishings—some that could double as pieces of artwork—that matched the home's architecture. "Come with me, please."

Tess gave the man a grim smile. "I'm sorry, no can do." She had a rule about this kind of situation. If she didn't know where she was and who was in charge, she remained close to the exit. "I'll wait here."

The man looked a tad worried. "He wouldn't like that."

"Who is he?" Tess asked.

"My employer."

Tess rolled her eyes. This was getting nuts. Forget Damien's orders. If he wanted to have this guy's art or whatever the man was selling, then he could get it himself.

Perhaps sensing that she was ready to bolt, "Danny" said in a hopeful voice, "If you could wait one moment, Ms. York?"

Tess released a breath. "Okay. But seriously, this had better get clear real soon."

Like a fretful mouse, the man scurried away, through the double-height living room and its beautiful floor-to-ceiling soapstone fireplace. Tess started counting to sixty. She got to fifty-one before she heard the butler returning.

But it wasn't the butler.

She heard him before she saw him, and her gut went tight. "Giving the help a hard time, are you Tess?"

Tess watched him walk toward her, the master of the manor, dressed in jeans and a black sweater, looking too gorgeous, too dangerous for words.

She shook her head as he approached. "Your house, huh? I should've guessed." She pointed a finger at him. "And, for the record, I wasn't trying to give anyone a hard time. I was being firm. But maybe he's not used to strong women coming here."

"Olin," he said, walking into the living room. "His name is Olin."

Tess followed. "Right. Well, maybe Olin's not used to you having strong women around."

Damien's eyes were cool and brilliant blue as he sat in a black leather armchair. "Only one woman comes here, and she's plenty strong."

"Only one, huh? How progressive of you," she said sarcastically, taking the chair across from him.

"You met her today, in fact."

"Wanda?" Tess said.

He nodded. "She's a good friend."

"How nice."

"I don't bring the women I date here."

The women. Plural. So, there were many. Of course there were many. She pushed away the nip of jealously in her gut and got down to business. "Why am I here, Damien? And with all the mystery?"

"Mystery?" he repeated.

She put her hand up. "No, forget it. I don't need an answer for that. I get it. You wanted me to see your amazing spread, how well you've done—and I have. It's fantastic, you're successful. Okay?" When he said nothing, just looked mildly amused, she pressed on. "Now, I have a job to do—one that was forced on me—and I'd like to get it done as soon as possible."

"I didn't have Wanda tell you that it was my house

you were coming to because I assumed you'd still be pretty pissed off at me and you'd probably stand me up. And I needed you to see this house so you could see my style, what I wanted for the red house."

Oh. Well, that made a small amount of sense. "You want the red house to go modern? It's a cozy little cottage."

"Cozy cottages can and should have modern touches."

"Fine. Okay. Cozy, but modern it is." She stood. "If I could get my coat, I need to go over to the motel and check in before it gets dark—"

"No."

She stared at him, puzzled. "No, what?," she said, laughing. "I don't get my coat back?"

"You're not staying at the motel, Tess."

"Excuse me?"

"No motels or hotels."

This guy was something else. "Where am I supposed to stay, then?"

Damien sat back in his chair.

Tess crossed her arms over her chest. "If you think I'm going to stay here, then the LA smog has really rotted your—"

"No. You're not staying here."

Her hands balled into fists, and she said through gritted teeth, "What do you suggest, then? Building an igloo?"

"You'll stay in the red house." He said it as though it was the simplest, most logical solution in the world.

Her stomach churned with irritation. "The red house is filthy and unfurnished."

"You'll change that."

Nostrils flaring with anger, Tess stood there, her body rigid. She wanted to scream at him, maybe clock him with that mean left hook she'd learned in self-defense class at the Y. But that was just what he wanted—a mad, frustrated, vulnerable Tess York.

Not going to happen.

"So, more punishment, is that it?" she said tightly.

A slow smile pulled at his lips.

Tess nodded. "Have at it, Sauer. Just know that when this is all done and you're back in California making another million, the only thing that'll have changed on this end will be that small amount of regret I felt when I walked out on you."

His gaze flashed with icy contempt. "It's getting dark. I'll have Olin get your coat."

"Don't bother." She left him standing there and walked to the entryway. After pulling her coat from the stainless steel closet, she left.

Every weekend for one year, Damien had come to Tribute to supervise the building of his hilltop house. It was everything he'd ever wanted, a twelve-thousand-square-foot glass house; a modern, mini-malist fortress that overlooked the little red house he couldn't let go of. He had designed the house so that he could see the red cottage from nearly every window. It was how he'd wanted it, needed it.

Whenever he looked down at it, he was reminded of her, and the feeling of betrayal had spurred him on, had made him wise and passionless and highly successful in business.

Damien took the elevator to the roof and stepped out on the deck. Snow was falling in sweet, tiny flakes, melting at once as they hit the heated stone floor. He could see for miles from up there, but he didn't even try to look beyond the borders of Tribute. His gaze rested where it always did—on the red house. A tiny speck of a place that mocked him big-time.

Right now it was dark. Obviously, she wasn't back yet.

"Sir?"

"Yes?" Damien didn't turn around to address Olin.

"Dinner is ready, sir."

"Nothing for me tonight."

Olin paused for a moment, then uttered a quick, "Yes, sir," before he disappeared.

Damien wasn't hungry. Not for food, at any rate. What he wanted was her. Her body and her soul. He wanted to make her hate him, then make her love him, then crush her as she'd crushed him.

And, after their meeting earlier, it looked as though he was well on his way….

"Seriously?"

Ruby Deets looked suitably remorseful as she shook her head, her platinum-blond beehive shifting as she moved. "I'm sorry, hon. Wish there was something I could do for you."

Starving and running out of the half cup of patience she had remaining, Tess leaned against Ruby's front desk. "You can. You can give me a room."

"Can't."

"He doesn't own you."

"No, that's true." Ruby leaned in, her double chin just hovering above the tarnished welcome bell. "But he does own the motel."

Tess grit her teeth. Of course he did.

"Is the grocery store still open?" she asked.

Ruby checked the clock on the wall. "You got another thirty minutes."

"Okay, thanks."

"You must've done something to really piss him off," Ruby remarked dryly.

"He's a man," Tess said, then turned to leave, calling over her shoulder, "They're not that hard to piss off."

Three hours later Tess sat on a blanket from her car in the red house's tiny living room. After she'd gotten rid of the cobwebs, scrubbed down the walls and mopped the floor in the one room, she'd built a fire in the brick fireplace and opened her deli sandwich and chips.

Between the rough accommodations and all the thoughts running through her brain, from Damien to the remodel to her past, she was not going to be sleeping much tonight.

For about a half a second, she'd contemplated going home and just explaining to Olivia what she was up against. Her partner was pretty understanding and very cool. No doubt, she'd pat Tess on the back, whip up a five-course meal—three of them heavy on the chocolate—then suggest they find a new office building immediately.

Oh, such a tempting thought.

But Tess was no coward, no quitter. She would take control of this situation and turn the red house into a comfortably modern masterpiece. Then, when the two weeks were up, she'd pack up and go home, put Damien behind her for good.

She took another bite of her egg salad sandwich. To make this work, she would have to stay one step ahead of him, try to anticipate what he would throw at her next. Because if there was one thing she could be sure of, it was that Damien Sauer had plans for her. Possibly destructive plans, and she had to be ready.

Four

"Bed's in the trunk, Tess."

"Thanks, Mr Opp." Tess pulled several hundred-dollar bills from the envelope stash. It was close to four in the afternoon and she was pretty wiped. She'd been cleaning since sunup. Later, on a trip into town for a late lunch, she had found the name and address of a man who sold handmade furnishings and gifts. She'd purchased a beautiful walnut bed, complete with mattress and box spring, as well as a few other pieces for the living room that she was going to pick up later in the week.

Mr. Opp took the money and gave Tess a tired grin. He was a tall, lanky man in his early seventies, who had a pack of little dogs that continually weaved their way in and out of his legs whenever he stopped to talk. "How about a few more sheets of *lefsa*? Butter and sugar on top?"

"No, thanks," Tess said graciously, eyeing the stack of round, flat potato bread. A half hour earlier she had made quite a dent in that stack. "I don't think I could eat another bite."

He grinned and said kindly, "I'll wrap up a few for the road, then."

"I'd appreciate that." With the limited selection of food in Tribute, she wasn't about to decline the offer. Especially when the food in question was ridiculously delicious.

She gave Mr. Opp another round of thank-yous, then got in her car and took off. As she drove back to the little red house, she felt better, as though she might be getting a handle on the situation. After last night and sleeping on the hardwood floor, just the thought of having a bed to sleep on tonight was a massive improvement. Sure, it was going to take every ounce of muscle she had to lug the thing inside and set it up, as Mr. Opp had no delivery service, but hey, it would be worth it.

The sun was settling itself into the horizon when she pulled into the driveway. Before bringing in the bed, she decided to grab some firewood from the side of the house first. She'd kept the heat on all day, but as she'd discovered last night, it wasn't the greatest source of warmth in the world.

After piling four logs into her arms, she pushed the front door open with her hip and went inside.

Immediately she felt something strange. She bent and gently rolled the logs to the floor, trying not to be too noisy. Her heart started pounding against the walls of her chest, but she wasn't sure why.

Was someone in the house? Something?

Animal or human?

She glanced around for something to use as a weapon. No baseball bat, and the chopping ax was outside beside the woodpile. Without thinking, she grabbed one of the logs, swung it back over her right shoulder. Her throat tight with nerves, she moved cautiously through the living room. This was crazy, she thought, stepping into the kitchen and flipping on the lights. There was nothing here, probably just her imagination.

But she let her guard down too quickly. As her arm fell to her side, someone seized her, grabbed her around the waist and spun her, then pinned her back against the countertop. The log dropped to the floor and made a crashing sound. Tess screamed, thrashed around until she saw who was holding her. Then she stopped cold and stared at him. "You!"

His face just inches from hers, Damien Sauer whispered, "Making yourself at home."

"You scared the hell out of me!" she said caustically, trying to break free of his grasp.

But Damien didn't release her. "And you almost knocked my head off my shoulders with that log."

"What a tragedy that would be," she said sarcastically.

Amusement glittered in his eyes. "You seem testy today."

"Do I?"

"Living in the lap of luxury not agreeing with you?"

"Living here is fine. It's the unwelcome guests I have a problem with."

"Then you should keep the door locked."

She ignored the truth in that statement. "What are you doing here? Aren't you supposed to be watching me jump and squirm from under that ten-thousand-square-foot magnifying glass you got up there?"

"Twelve thousand."

"What?"

"Twelve thousand square feet."

She rolled her eyes. He was one of the most arrogant, self-centered…

"I'm checking in," he said, his sapphire gaze moving over her face. "On my wife."

A ripple of laughter escaped her. "That arrangement is going on only in your head."

He leaned in, his mouth just inches from her. "And in your partners' heads, as well, right?"

How was it possible to want to kill someone and kiss them at the same time? They stood there, so close, the scent of snow and leather emanating from Damien as he baited her with his words and his full lips.

Ignoring the prickly warm sensation inside her breasts, she forced her gaze to meet his. "I want you to let me go now."

At her words, something changed in his expression. It was no longer playful, more serious, and he released her, backed up, even walked away into the living room. For a moment Tess just remained there, her back against the butcher-block countertop. She'd said those exact words to another man many years ago and many times before, but with very different results. Damien confused her. He wanted to punish her, yet his punishment was all mental…

With a quick breath, she followed him into the living room. "As you can see, I've cleaned the place. That's about as far as I've gotten in the one day I've been here. Oh, that and I bought a bed."

"A bed?"

"If I'm staying here it's at least going to be tolerably comfortable."

"Where is it?"

"In the car."

He was opening the front door and disappearing outside before Tess got a clue about what he was doing. "I don't need your help, Damien," she called, running after him into the frosty cold air of twilight time. "In fact, I don't need anything from you, except maybe…"

A foot from her car, he paused and turned around. "Except what?"

From three to five in the morning last night, she'd given this idea much thought. Damien wasn't going to be the only beneficiary in this deal. Tess didn't do things that way anymore. "I'd like you to promise me something."

He raised a brow.

"After I do this job, you'll sell the Minneapolis building."

He crossed his arms over his chest. "Which building is that?"

She cocked her head to the side. "Don't be obtuse."

For a moment he just stared at her, looking both emotionally and physically cold, puffs of warm air escaping his mouth. Then he turned around and walked to the back of her car. He had the trunk popped and the headboard out in seconds. "You didn't lock your car door, either?"

"I didn't think this was chop shop alley, Damien."

He carried the headboard up the walk, and Tess followed him. "The building I'm referring to is the one that houses No Ring Required. I want you to sell it."

"Why should I?" He put the headboard inside, then went back for more.

Again, she followed after him like a hungry puppy as he removed parts of the bed frame from her SUV and brought them inside. "Because it's the right thing to do, and underneath that badass exterior you're a good guy."

"No, seriously, why should I?" he said dryly, returning to the car and hauling out the mattress and box spring.

"Because I'm willing to walk away from this if you don't."

He snorted. "You wouldn't. I know you—"

"You know nothing about me, Damien!" She said the words so loudly, so passionately, he stopped in the doorway and stared at her.

She shook her head. "You have no idea who I am now. What I've…" She needed to go easy here. "What I've seen and experienced in the past six years. I'm willing to let you humiliate me, give orders and use me for the next two weeks, to protect my business and my partners. But I won't do it for longer than that."

He didn't move. His chin was set and his eyes narrowed.

She walked to him, her tone low and cool. "You clearly don't need the money. And after we're done here, I'd think you'd want to put me back in the past where I belong."

"That easy?"

"Yes." She held out her hand. "Okay?"

Damien didn't speak for a moment, then he reached out and took her hand in his.

The warmth of his hand instantly seeped into her body, her bones, and for just a second a flash of the past came roaring into her mind. She saw herself in Damien's arms in this very house, saw him kissing her neck, then her mouth.

She pulled her hand away, knowing her cheeks burned. "If you're done here, I have work to do."

He nodded darkly. "I'm done." He walked past her, down the path.

Then she noticed something. "Hey, how did you get here? I didn't see a car."

He glanced over his shoulder. "Walked."

She couldn't stop herself from asking, "You want a ride back? It's kind of far."

He shook his head. "No. It's just far enough."

He disappeared down the street and into the darkness so quickly she didn't get a chance to ask him what he'd meant by that.

Damien arrived home hungry and cold as hell. But all in all, the walk had been a good one. Time to clear his head, make new plans and fill his lungs with clean air. Couldn't do that in Los Angeles.

Olin was hovering at the front door when Damien walked in. "Sir?"

"You look panicked, Olin."

He took Damien's coat and tossed it gently over his arm. "Mrs. Roth is here and she brought along a Mr. Kaplan."

Damien checked his watch. "It's eight o'clock."

"I told them it was too late, but they insisted on waiting." The man leaned in and whispered covertly, "Mrs. Roth called Mr. Kaplan a land developer."

Damien chuckled. "Yes, I know who he is. How long have they been here?"

"Twenty minutes." Olin stood taller. "I'll go back and tell them you don't wish to be—"

"No. I'd told Irene to come by anytime." He should've specified anytime during the day. But this was a special circumstance, part of his plan, and he couldn't afford to be his usual overly demanding self. "Tell them I'll be right there."

"Yes, sir."

"Where are they?"

"The study."

"Fine." He started up the stairs.

"Sir?"

Damien turned. "Yes, Olin?"

"I know it's not my business to ask, but if you're thinking of selling this house, I would be most grateful to know—"

"I'm not selling."

"Oh."

"Not this house, anyway."

There were times when Tess York believed she didn't feel anything—that the ugliness and shame of her past had made her numb. Then, out of the blue, she'd get a few gentle waves of emotion. They were normally accompanied by memories, not good ones, but even so, the waves did remind her that she was still alive and able to feel. And she had to take that as a positive.

Tonight Tess sat on the new bed and rubbed oil onto the snakelike skin of her inner thigh. She was riding a wave right now, where the reality of the massive burn scar that Henry had inflicted that last night before she'd left him was meeting up with the emotions of the memory. It was an odd thing, too, because she always felt the scar, felt her jeans rub against it or the shower water pummeling it.

Tonight, however, it burned.

She couldn't help thinking it was Damien's presence in her life again, the notion that if she had picked him, her life might've been so different—that this scar wouldn't have existed. But who was to know. In his own way, Damien had turned out to be a monster, too.

Outside, snow started to fall. Tomorrow was a big day, the real renovation could begin.

Tess put her salve away, got under the covers and closed her eyes.

Five

The trouble with picking a paint color was twofold:
too many choices, then there was the what-if-this-
looks-hideous-on-the-wall factor. Normally Tess
could get past these minor roadblocks in about fifteen
minutes. In her five years with NRR, she'd chosen
color for over a hundred walls, but this morning she'd
been at Hardy's Hardware for an hour, unable to
make a decision.

Tess stood in front of the paint chips and stared at
the blur of color, a shiny bald-headed Frank Hardy
beside her. She shook her head. "I just don't know."

"You could go white," Frank suggested.

"True…"

"What's the plan for the house?"

"I'm not sure." Maybe that was part of the problem here—no clear goal. Damien still hadn't told her what he was going to do with the house after she fixed it up.

Frank took a chip labeled Basic Eggshell off the board and held it out for her. "Neutral is good."

Sure. Good, but kind of boring. "The thing is, Frank, the man who owns the house is just not a neutral guy, and it's not a neutral house."

"Do I know this guy?"

"Probably."

"Who is it?" Impatience with the nutty woman was starting to register on his face. "Maybe if I knew who you were working for I could be a better help to you."

Maybe, but she wasn't experiencing the greatest luck with the people in town who knew she was working for Damien. Best to keep that information to herself. "I think I'm just going to go for it." She started handing over paint chips. "I'll take the Ryegrass for the kitchen, Toasty and Svelte and Sage for living room and dining room, Buttercream for the bathroom and Ramie for the bedroom."

He looked relieved. "And the exterior will have to wait for warmer weather."

"Yes. But even then, the house will always remain red."

The man's voice came from behind them, and both Tess and Frank turned to see Damien standing there. He looked very tall under the store's low ceiling and very handsome in jeans, black sweater and wool coat.

"For a project that's supposed to be done by me and only me, you're around an awful lot," Tess said, only mildly irritated. "What are you doing here?"

"I'm in dire need of a rake," he said with complete seriousness, walking toward her.

"Yeah, right. You were spying on my paint choices."

Damien smiled lazily. "I'd like to see what I'm getting for my money."

Tess gave him a look of mock disgust. "Where's the trust, dude?"

His brows went up: "Dude?"

Sticking out his hand in Damien direction, Frank grinned. "So, you're the not-so-neutral guy, huh?"

Damien shook it and grinned. "She was talking about me?"

"Didn't know it was you, but now that I do, I get it."

"Get what?" Tess asked Frank.

Frank shrugged, stuffed his hands into the pockets of his stained overalls. "Why it took you so long to decide. Mr. Sauer does that to all the ladies."

Tess snorted. "What? Make them crazy?"

"In a word, yup."

Tess cocked her head to the side and said in a high, breathy, girlie voice, "Well, I just can't decide anything, you make me too crazy."

Frank burst out laughing, pointing at Tess. "I like her."

"Yeah." Damien's sapphire gaze moved over her face in a hungry, possessive way, sending an electrifying jolt of awareness right into Tess's core. It had been so long since she'd felt something stir her up that way. She hardly remembered how good it was to feel turned on. How unfortunate it was that the man who had done the stirring was also the man who wanted to punish her, then put her behind him and forget she ever existed.

Frank cleared his throat. "All right. Give me a half hour for the six gallons."

Tess thanked him, then walked outside with Damien beside her. It was a crisp, winter morning with just enough sun to make being outside moderately tolerable. From lampposts to street signs to shop windows, the town was dressed for Christmas, and, feeling in pretty good spirits that day, Tess suggested they take a walk down the sidewalk to enjoy the sights.

As Damien walked beside her, he said, "I stopped by the house."

She was about to ask him once again about his ongoing involvement in the renovation but decided against it. He was here, in town, and had made himself involved. He was a man who did what he wanted and got what he wanted. Trying to stop him would surely prove fruitless.

"And how's the drywall looking?" she asked.

"Satisfactory. I see you found Jamie and Max."

She nodded. "Best drywallers in the county."

"So they say," he said as they rounded the corner. "Where are you off to now?"

"I have a date."

He came to a dead stop on the sidewalk. "What?"

His eyes were fierce and practically black as he stared down at her.

A shiver of satisfaction moved through her at his reaction. But she mentally flicked it away. "I have a date with a flooring salesperson."

She watched him process this information, then make a satisfied grunt before continuing down the street. "Driving into Jackson?"

"Yep. They have a flooring outlet there. I'm thinking maybe some prefab oak."

He sniffed imperiously. "Prefab? No. Absolutely not."

She looked him over. "You know, you've turned into quite the snob, Sauer."

"Why? Because I like good quality, natural materials?"

"Prefab can be really nice."

"I only want the best materials used on this house."

"Why?" A sudden gust of snowy wind assaulted her, and she pulled the collar of her coat tighter around her neck. "What is the plan for this house, Damien? I mean, correct me if I'm wrong, but if you're going to do your thing and flip it, isn't the rule to put in the best product for the cheapest price?"

Damien was quiet for a moment, then he said neutrally, "I won't be flipping the house."

Okay. So, he wasn't selling. Why did that make her feel so relieved? Why did that make her feel anything at all?

The town was small, and soon they ran out of

sidewalk and shops, and they were headed into the park. Neither one of them suggested turning back, and as they neared an abandoned, snow-covered swing set, Tess turned off the path and made a beeline for the swings. She brushed off the tuft of snow covering the plastic red seat and sat. Damien stood nearby and watched her swing back and forth gently.

"If you could choose anything for the floors," he said evenly. "Never mind the cost, what would you choose?"

"You mean, my fantasy floor?"

He nodded.

She thought for a moment, then sighed. "Oh, let's see. Probably, thick planks, antique wood, maybe barn wood."

He nodded. "Okay."

"Okay, what?"

"Do it."

She laughed, continuing to swing back and forth even though it was starting to make her nauseous. "That kind of floor can run twenty dollars a square foot."

"Just order it, but make sure it's here at the end of the week."

"That's impossible."

"Nothing's impossible. Pay whatever they ask for the shipping and they'll get it here in a week." His cell phone rang and he glanced at the number, seemed to deem it unimportant and slipped it back in his coat pocket. "In fact, I want you to pick everything for the house with no thought to the cost. Make all your choices fantasy choices."

She put her feet down and skidded to a stop. "Come on, Damien."

"What?"

"Make all the choices fantasy ones? To what end?"

"I'm not following."

She shook her head. "I don't get this. What are you doing?"

"Is there something wrong with enjoying your work?"

This went past enjoying her work. "Is this some show of how much money you have?"

His eyes narrowed. "I don't put on shows."

"You have to know that I'm not interested in your money and what it can buy. It doesn't impress me. It means nothing to me. Less than nothing."

He laughed bitterly. "I find that hard to believe."

"What does that mean?" she demanded.

"It's why you went with a man you didn't love."

"What?"

"Henry offered you security," he said, walking over to her. "With him you believed your future would be set, financially and otherwise. Isn't that true?"

"Yes, it's true."

"And what did I offer you?" He stood before her, his face taut, his gaze searching hers. "Not much—just a hope for a future."

"Do we really need to do this?" She pushed herself off of the swing. The paint was probably done.

Without another word, she walked past Damien. But she didn't get very far.

"And now look at us," he called after her. "Your future, your security is in my hands."

She stopped, just feet away. The past wouldn't rest as long as there were others still living in it. And Damien clearly was. He sounded so cruel, so unhappy, so delighted. It was disgusting and foolish, and she couldn't stop herself from turning around and walking right back up to him. When she was there, in his face, her breathing unsteady and her jaw trembling, she blurted it out. "Do you want to know why I went with him? Why I left you?"

"Yes."

"I loved him, Damien."

"I don't believe you."

She said the words slowly. "I was in love with him."

His jaw was clenched so tight she thought it might snap. "You were in love with what you thought he could give you."

"It's all the same."

"No, it's not."

"How would you know?"

She turned around to go, but he grabbed her arm and pulled her back to face him. "If you loved him, what was it you felt for me?"

She lifted her chin. "Lust."

His eyes darkened with rage. "Then you won't mind this."

She didn't have time to react as he leaned in and covered her mouth with his, his free hand cupping her nape.

His kiss was hard, punishing, and she wanted to be repelled by it, by him, but she wasn't. Every muscle, every inch of her skin trembled and ached. Yes, it had been a long time since she was touched this way, but it wasn't that, it was Damien. He was an artist, always had been. The way he held her, his lips taking greedily one moment, then pulling back to nibble and slowly suckle.

Tess sagged against him, her fists wrapped around the collar of his coat, her hips pressing into his thigh.

Her pulse slapped against her rib cage. She wanted more, so much more. If only they were back at the red house, not outside in the park....

Delicious, mind-numbing heat quickly turned to anxiety as she realized where she was and what she was doing and who had started it all. She released him, pushing him away as she stepped back. Her brain felt foggy and she shook her head.

"That will not happen again." She didn't look at him, couldn't, her body was still humming.

This time when she turned and walked away, he didn't reach out to stop her. But his words echoed through the snow-covered park, a dark, delicious warning...

"Don't be so sure."

"Slow down, Damien, for heaven's sake."

"I'm fine."

"You're going to choke." Her hands planted on her formidable hips, Wanda Bennett watched Damien devour the plate of food she'd just set in front of him. Inside her food store, there was a diner counter where she served the basics, from grilled cheese to pancakes. It all depended on her mood. Today her mood had run in the direction of everything egg related. Eggs weren't really high on Damien's list of favorite foods, but he never tried to persuade Wanda to do anything else but exactly what she wanted to do. She was just like him, arrogant and stubborn as hell. If there weren't such a difference in the colors of their skin, he might wonder if they were related.

"Aren't you going to Minneapolis this afternoon?" she asked him.

"Yes." He had a four-o'clock meeting with an investor. "I have to be at the airport in twenty minutes."

"Why aren't you eating on the plane, then?"

He shrugged.

"Steak and champagne is a helluva lot better than my greasy egg sandwich."

"No, it's not," he said sullenly.

She glared at him expectantly. "What's the problem? Is it the girl? The redhead?"

Damn right it was the girl. Always that girl. Why couldn't he be done with her? Why couldn't he have stopped himself from going there, kissing her, tasting her. Now all he wanted was more. "I need a napkin. Or a hose."

Wanda ignored him. "Yeah, I figured she wasn't just an employee. But she's not really your type, either."

"I don't have a type."

"No? I suppose it's just a coincidence that every woman who's ever followed you up here has weighed less than a toothbrush with a figure to match. And," she pointed out dramatically, "I swear a couple of them have shown up on the covers of those rag mags over by the register." Wanda shook her head. "Never understood why a man like you would take company with women who don't know their nose from their elbows...but it's none of my affair."

"No, it's not." He stood and tossed money on the counter. "Truth is, Wanda, those women are wonderfully uncomplicated. No strings, no—"

"No real feelings?" she interrupted.

Damien shot her a defensive look. "I have to go."

She pressed her lips together and shrugged. "Okay, go."

Wanda was the one woman in his life who never pressed him for anything more than what he wanted to give. "She is my past," he said with far too much irritation. "She made me what I am."

A slow smile touched Wanda's full lips. "And what is that?"

"A soulless, uncompromising pain in the ass."

She grinned broadly. "A devil in the bedroom and in the boardroom?"

Damien's brow lifted, and he matched her grin with one of his own. "You'd never marry me, would you?"

"If you were ten years younger...maybe."

He leaned over the counter and gave her a peck on the cheek. "It's supposed to snow tonight. Be careful going home."

* * *

It was nearly midnight, but the last thing Tess felt like doing was sleeping. She was running on Double Stuff Oreos and diet cola, and had just finished the demo of the kitchen and bathroom floors, removing all the old tiles. The installers were coming tomorrow with the antique hand-hewn limestone she'd found through Frank at the hardware store.

She cranked up the stereo she'd bought that afternoon. She had a thing for eighties music, especially Prince, and as she poured the old tiles from the dustpan into the garbage can and hauled them outside, she danced. She was in the middle of the living-room, on her last load of tile, when it happened. The floorboard beneath her creaked, then cracked, then suddenly gave way.

She had no time to react as her slipper-clad foot dropped through the subflooring. For a moment she just stood there, one foot on the floor, the other in a hole.

"Damn dry rot," she muttered, dropping onto her backside and easing her foot out. But as she did, the pain came on fast. Then she noticed her slipper had fallen off, and her naked foot was sporting a good deal of blood. Confused, she cupped her foot and rotated it so she could see the ball and heel, find the source of the blood. Her stomach clenched when she saw it. There was a nasty-looking gash on the ball of her foot.

"Crap." She took off her other slipper and pressed the soft side against the open cut, then she hobbled to the bedroom where she kept the emergency kit.

After cleaning the wound with hydrogen peroxide, she grabbed a butterfly Band-Aid. She tried to get the cut to close well, but every time she moved, it hurt like hell and blood seeped out everywhere.

She was going to need stitches. How in the world was she going to make that happen?

"Tess?"

Her heart leaped into her throat as fear gripped her. Then she recognized the voice, and relief spread through her. Before this moment, she'd never thought she'd be so happy to hear his voice. "I'm in here, Damien—the master bedroom."

He walked in, looking cold, tired and thoroughly pissed off. "Are you completely insane?"

"Is that a serious question?"

"It's after midnight and the front door is wide open."

"I was working."

"If I hadn't been driving by—" Then he saw the blood on her foot, on the slipper, on the floor. "What the hell happened to you?"

"Rotting floorboard."

"I saw it when I came in, but I thought it was demo." He squatted down and inspected her foot.

"I think I sliced it on the edge of the board next to the one that gave way, or maybe there was something sharp on the subflooring—I don't know."

"Did you clean it with anything?"

"Yes and I tried a butterfly bandage, but nothing's stopping the blood. I think I need to go to the emergency room."

He got up and went to the bathroom, came back with a roll of toilet paper. He used nearly the whole thing, but in seconds he had her entire instep wrapped up like the foot of a mummy.

She gave him a nod and a smile. "Thanks."

"Sure." Then without warning, he lifted her up and gathered her into his arms.

"What are you doing?"

"Taking you to the emergency room," he said, walking out of the bedroom.

"I can call—"

"Get serious." He stepped around the rotting floorboard and walked out the door. "An ambulance takes forever. I'm here and I'm taking you."

"Are you sure this won't mess up your plans to punish me?" she said dryly. "You know, by actually helping me?"

His jaw tightened as they headed for the black sedan in the driveway. "You got hurt on my watch. There's nothing else to say. Now, just shut up and put your arms around my neck, you're starting to slip."

Six

As Tess sat in a plastic chair in the cold half-empty emergency room, Damien paced. Waiting was not his strong suit. Sure, there were a few other people in the E.R., but none of them had anything too serious going on, none of them belonged to him, and none of them made his gut tighten with just a look.

Anger bubbled up in his blood, and he searched the room for someone who looked as though they wanted a good verbal sparring match. But no one would make eye contact with him.

"You look like a caged animal, Damien. Sit down."

He stopped and stared at Tess. He hadn't noticed

before but she was wearing a pair of red flannel Christmas pajamas and her hair was piled on top of her head, a few wavy strands falling about her neck and shoulders. Not surprisingly, she still wore the one remaining black slipper. She was a mess, but a very sexy mess.

He scowled at her. "Are you keeping pressure on your foot?"

"Yes. Now sit down. You look nuts."

"I look nuts?" he said, ire in his tone. "You want to know what's nuts?"

"I'm guessing that's a rhetorical question," she said, her makeup-free face looking very, very beautiful, yet very pale.

His voice dropped to a whisper. "Nuts is wearing slippers during demolition."

"It was late."

He threw his hands in the air. "You were knocking out tiles."

"I wore boots for that part."

"Well, why the hell didn't you keep them on for the cleanup? What did you do when you went outside?"

"I have duck shoes outside the front door. I slipped into those."

He groaned. "Women."

"We're great aren't we?" She gave him an innocent smile. "Complicated, mysterious…"

"That's not where I was going."

Her smile suddenly evaporated, and she closed her eyes and sucked air through her teeth.

Switching from anger to concern, Damien dropped down beside her. "Does it hurt?"

"Not any worse than a tooth extraction," she muttered through gritted teeth. "Without the pain meds, of course."

He cursed. "I'll be right back." He stalked over to the front desk and spoke to the nurse, "That woman with the cut foot needs to see someone right away."

Staring at a patient chart, the nurse didn't even look up at him. "We're busy tonight, sir. She'll have to wait."

"It doesn't look all that busy to me," he said with a thread of irritation running through his tone. "There's a guy in here with a cold, and another guy who's too drunk to even fill out his paperwork. The woman I brought in is bleeding."

The nurse looked up then and shrugged. "I'm sorry. Rules are rules."

Screw rules. Damien took out his cell phone and, right there at the reception desk, punched in a number.

"Sir, please go outside to use your cell phone," said the nurse.

Damien ignored her. The phone rang three times before it was picked up.

"Hello."

"Greg, it's Damien Sauer."

"Damien?" came the tired male voice. "Everything all right?"

"Sorry to call this late, but I'm having an issue at your hospital."

"You're at the hospital? What happened?"

"Not me. A friend. She needs to see a doctor, but we're dealing with first come, first serve, and to be honest there are no emergencies ahead of us—"

The man cut him off. "I'll take care of it right now."

"Thanks."

"I'm sorry about this, Damien. I'm sure they would never have allowed this to happen if they knew who you were."

Damien hung up the phone with the president and CEO of Tribute Memorial Hospital, but he didn't move from the reception desk. Seconds later a call came through on the emergency room phone that sent everyone in a panic. The nurse who earlier had brushed him off now simultaneously blanched and smiled as she told Damien she'd be right with him, then rushed away with several other members of the hospital staff.

Thirty seconds later, two nurses and a doctor burst through the double doors with the cleanest of squeaky-clean wheelchairs, and Tess was whisked away to a private room.

"All right," Tess said to the male nurse who had lifted her from the wheelchair and was gently placing her on a bed. "What did he do?"

She was pointing at Damien, who only shrugged and said, "I'm going to find you some ice chips and the best wound specialist in this hospital."

He was just outside the door when he heard Tess say, "Seriously, did he threaten you guys?

The male nurse laughed. "No, miss."

"Then what's all the fuss?"

"The man who brought you in is Damien Sauer."

"I know."

"Then you also know that he donated the new emergency wing to the hospital?"

Tess sighed. "No, that part I didn't know."

Damien drove his car up the steep hill without hitting a rock, hard chunk of snow or pothole. Pretty damn impressive. Not that the woman next to him had noticed. She'd been asleep for the past ten minutes, the painkillers they'd given her at the hospital working their magic. But as he pulled into the garage and killed the engine, she stirred, her hands closing around her purse, a soft moan escaping her lips.

He looked over at her, lifted a brow. "Hey."

She turned to him, her eyes heavy and tired. "Hi." Her foot was wrapped in a bandage and in his trunk was the pair of crutches the hospital had given them. "Where are we?" she asked.

"You're staying with me."

Tess came awake immediately, even sat up a little in her seat. "No."

"Don't be an ass, Tess. You heard the doctor. You need to stay off your foot for a few days."

"Not here."

"You need the help."

"I don't," she said defiantly. "I can handle this myself."

"How?"

She paused, then let her head fall back against the seat. "Fine, I need help." She rubbed a hand over her face. "But I'll get it from someone else."

"Who?"

"I'll go home, back to Minneapolis. You can get someone to finish the job."

There was no way he was letting her out of his life just yet. He needed so much from her: to make her love him again; to feel her mouth again; to leave her cold like she'd left him. "I don't want anyone else to finish the job." His voice grew dangerously low. "That wasn't our deal."

"Well, how do you think the house is going to get done? I won't be able to do anything major for at least two days. I have a tiling guy coming tomorrow to help me lay the tile, and there's no way—"

"I'll do it."

She stared at him. "What?"

"I'll help the guy lay tile. I've done it a hundred times."

"Not lately, I'm willing to bet."

"You think I can't get dirty?" Damien asked with a touch of heat.

Her mouth twitched with amusement and she returned bluntly, "No, I think you can definitely get dirty."

"Was that an insult or a sexual innuendo?"

She shrugged. "Who knows? Depends if it was me talking or the drugs."

He chuckled. "Perhaps a little of both. Now, tomorrow I'll meet the guy at...what time?"

"Eight," she supplied, looking unconvinced. "You sure you're up for all that manual labor now that you're Mr. Sauer, millionaire real estate mogul who donates hospital wings on a whim."

"That had nothing to do with a whim. That was a kick-ass tax deduction."

She looked at the ceiling. "Oh, that kind heart of yours, Damien."

Laughing again, he got out of the car and came around to her side. But when he got there, Tess was starting to fade a little. The twinkle in her eyes from a moment ago had disappeared, and she was sitting back against the seat, looking miserable. With supreme gentleness, he bent and slipped his hands underneath her. "I'm going to carry you."

"And I'm going to let you," she whispered.

"Pain's back?"

"With a vengeance and a hammer and some kind of hand-crank drill."

He shook his head, grinned. "You're the only one I know who can joke through their pain."

"Who's joking?"

He carried her into the house, through the living room and up the stairs to the second floor. He'd called ahead and had instructed Olin to fix up the room overlooking the garden. He'd never admit it to anyone but himself, but he'd had Tess in mind when he'd designed the room. It had a huge bed with a down comforter, a lavish bathroom and wall-to-wall windows. Even in the sea of pain she was riding, she smiled when she saw it.

"Nice room."

"It has a great view in the morning." He laid her on the bed, her back against the pillows.

She looked up at him. "Is this your room?"

"No."

"Then how do you know about the view in the morning?" She stopped herself, put a hand up. "Forget I asked."

He sat beside her. "What are you rambling on about?"

"Your stay in this room with your many guests. You have had women stay in here before, right?"

"Does it matter?"

Her face contorted with pain and she practically barked out the word, "No."

"All right. Relax now. Can I help you take off something?"

She smirked. "Cute."

A grin tugged at his mouth. She was something else, this one, he thought as he opened the bottle of pain medicine she'd been given at the hospital pharmacy. He took out a pill, then he handed her a bottle of water from the bedside table. "Take this."

"With pleasure." She popped the pill, drank the water, then sank back against the pillows, closing her eyes. After a moment her eyes drifted back open and they locked with his. "Hey."

"Hey."

"Thank you."

"For what?" He felt himself softening with her, and it killed him.

"Helping me out. It should just be the one night, then—"

"Stop, Tess."

But she wouldn't. "I'm a pretty quick healer. Tomorrow I should be a lot better, and I won't need to be watched over or—"

"I get it," he interrupted with an edge to his voice. "You don't want to rely on anyone." He reached over and pulled the covers up to her chin, then he stood. "Go to sleep now."

She nodded and closed her eyes, and Damien turned to leave.

Yes, he wanted to touch her again, make her need him, but he had to be vigilant. If he got too close, cared too much, there was a chance he might end up needing her again—and that he could not allow.

Tess was dreaming. It was one of those situations where she knew she was dreaming and she wanted to stay in it, and see it through to the end. She was dancing the tango in a competition, and her partner couldn't seem to hold her correctly. Every time he tried, she'd slip out of his arms. Around them, other couples dipped and stomped and made grand gestures with their arms, but Tess just stood there in the middle of it all, waiting,

waiting for this guy to get his act together and take her in his arms.

Not far away, at the judges' table, was Damien. He sat on a throne, a crown on his head, watching them, his eyes flared and his jaw set as though he found the whole thing repellent. As the music dissolved and the couples danced off the floor, Damien stood and walked toward her, his hand outstretched…

And then Tess opened her eyes. The music was gone, along with the activity and drama. She was in Damien's guest room and her foot was bandaged and it stung like the devil. She blinked, then glanced around. The curtains had been drawn on only one side of the massive windows, leaving the other side exposed. Outside, the sky was a bleak gray as if it was just too tired to contemplate morning….

Maybe in an hour or two, it seemed to say.

On the other side of the room, Damien was asleep in a chair by the fireplace. Tess's first reaction to seeing him there was to feel comforted by his presence. But that was no good, right? Comforted by the man who wanted her to suffer so he could get her out of his mind and his life? That mentality didn't sound like something she would ever be comfortable being around.

She just stared at him, a heart-stopping Adonis in a blue sweatshirt and jeans. Had he actually slept in that chair all night? she wondered. And why? Seriously, why was he even letting her stay at his house?

Why did he seem to despise her one moment, then treat her so gently the next?

Her gaze caught on something beside him on the floor. Her suitcase. He had gone back to the red house for her things. Her belly clenched. He was expecting her to remain there for more than a day.

She shifted in the bed, tried to get comfortable, but the bandage on her foot was awkward and the sting had morphed into a painful ache and stiffness.

Well, his expectations were going to be met, she thought. She wasn't going anywhere. A wave of panic moved into her already tight belly. She hated feeling stuck, feeling as though she were unable to get up and go, no matter how desperately she wanted to. It reminded her of those endless, or seemingly endless, days and nights in Henry's house, where he watched every move she made and pulled her back if she tried to put even a pinky toe across the line.

"You're awake."

Her head came up with a jerk. Damien was staring at her, so handsome, so devilish with his dark eyes and stubbled jaw. "I'm awake."

"You okay?"

"Can't sleep."

"Does your foot hurt?" He got up, came to sit beside her on the bed.

"Only if I move it."

"Then don't move it."

Her heart stuttered. Why did he look concerned? Was this just a way of helping her to get better faster, getting her back to work? Was he willing to be extra nice just to get her to finish the house?

As she downed two more pain pills, she thought about how her mind worked now. The belief that there was always a motive behind any action. She hated it. But wasn't there was always a motive with men?

She gestured to her bag on the floor. "Thanks for getting my stuff."

"Sure."

She took a deep breath. "You know, Damien. I'm not comfortable here."

"I know."

"With you taking care of me."

"I know."

"In fact, it makes me a little crazy."

A smile tugged at his mouth. "Too bad."

She returned his smile. "You should go back to your room, get some sleep."

He didn't move. His gaze raked over her face, then paused at her mouth. "Yeah, I probably should."

But instead he leaned in and kissed her.

Seven

Damien knew the moment he tasted her that he had just bought his ticket to hell.

Nothing—not even a bandaged, aching foot—was going to stop him from taking more. It was as if time had never passed. She smelled the same—that sweet, cool vanilla scent that had always driven him insane. He touched her face, her soft cheek, felt the skin tighten as she opened her mouth and deepened the kiss. The action tied him in knots, had his head pounding, his heart, too.

He dropped his head back, stared at her, into those large, hungry gray eyes. He'd never wanted anything more than he wanted her at that moment, and when she gave him a small, tentative smile, he crushed his mouth to hers, devouring the wet heat of her, changing angles with every breath, her long red curls tickling his face.

On a soft sigh, Tess placed her hands on either side of his head, her fingers snaking into his hair, forcing him closer.

Damien went hard as granite. This was going to be punishment for them both, pleasure for them both.

He ripped his mouth from hers and kissed her neck, nuzzling at the spot where her pulse pounded. She moaned and fisted his hair, tugging him closer. He nipped at her skin the way she used to love as his fingers madly searched for the buttons on her pajama top.

"Kiss me," she whispered. "Kiss me so I can't say no."

Her words excited him, yet were a warning, too—but he was too far gone to care. He wanted her mouth again, wanted to taste her tongue, suckle and bite and make her shiver, make her wet.

His mouth covered hers as his fingers flicked open the buttons on her top. He could hardly wait to feel her, that soft, milky skin beneath his palm. He cursed against her mouth as his hand slid beneath the flannel and over the full curve of her breast. She moaned and arched against him, and the sound filled him with longing. He liberated the buttons of her pajama top, then lowered his head and gently lapped at the soft peak, then again and again, circling the pink flesh until the nipple turned dark and hard.

Tess let her head fall back against the pillow as he continued in easy, lazy circles. Then, when his body and mind were about to explode, Damien took the hard bud into his mouth and suckled deeply. Again and again he suckled until Tess's mewling sounds turned to deep moans. He continued as he let one hand drift down her belly to the top of her pajama bottoms. Her reaction was quick. She stiffened and her hand came down over his.

His head came up and he looked at her.

She swallowed, shook her head. "It's…it's my foot. Hurts."

He turned away. "Dammit. I'm sorry." He felt like a giant ass. What kind of man hit on a woman in pain? Maybe the kind who was only looking for a little payback. He stood. "I'm gonna go."

"Back to bed?"

Not a chance. "I'm going to the red house. Get things set up for the tile job."

"It's so early."

"By the time I get there the sun will be up."

"Okay."

He raised a brow at her. "You're not to move."

"Damien…"

"If you need anything," he said, his body feeling as tight as a jackhammer. "Olin is here, and you just have to call down."

"I'll be going to the ladies' room alone," she said with a half smile.

"Of course." He walked over to the fireplace and

grabbed her crutches. "Use these only if absolutely necessary."

"Yes, sir." She gave him a mock salute.

"Now, if you get bored, there's some books on the nightstand here, and—" he gestured to the large trunk at the end of the bed "—there's a television in there. You just have to use the remote."

"Seriously?" she asked, surprised.

He nodded.

"It's inside the trunk?"

"Yes."

"Fancy."

She sat there, in bed, her cheeks flushed, her hair tousled and sexy and Damien felt as if he was going to explode.

Too damn much already. He couldn't stare at her for one more second. He turned around and walked out of the room, calling over his shoulder, "I'll be back around noon."

Once upon a time, a rabbit was caught in a trap. It sat there for hours until it felt as though it was going quite mad, then it proceeded to gnaw its foot off. Yes, it was bleeding and in pain as it limped through the forest, but it was free.

With her crutches tucked under her arms, Tess explored the second floor. It was all she could do. No up and no down. She had ruled out the stairs, as she had easily envisioned herself falling down them and being bedridden in Damien's ultramodern house long after he'd returned to California.

Slow and steady, she walked down the hallway, past a few more bedrooms, then a workout room and a billiard room. None of these rooms did anything to pique her curiosity. But then, at the very end of the house, in a large, square-shaped room, she saw a library. Heavy on charm, the space was lined in books and artwork. The furniture was a mixture of leather and chenille, and in the middle of one wall, a river-rock fireplace.

Perfect. A lively blaze danced in the fireplace, and after Tess grabbed a few random novels from the shelf, she sat in front of the fireplace on the brown leather couch.

As she was relaxing, her foot propped up on the coffee table, she saw something move out of the corner of one eye. She turned to see the man she had dubbed "Danny Devito" enter the room.

He inclined his head. "Good morning, Miss York."

"Hi, there. Olin, right?"

"Yes, miss."

"Good, because I wanted to apologize for the other day. I was pretty rude."

Olin shook his head. "No, miss."

"Oh, c'mon, Olin, it's okay. You can say it."

The man smiled, but it was a very thin-lipped one, as though he were fighting the urge to laugh. "You seemed…frustrated."

"I was. But I'm sure that's not the first time you've

seen a frustrated woman—you know, with who your boss is and everything."

Olin's smile faded. "Can I get you something, miss? Breakfast? Coffee?"

"No, thank you."

"I could help you back to the room, if you wish."

Boy, she knew where this was headed. "Thanks, Olin. But I'm good here."

Olin's brown eyes were filled with nervous energy. "It's just that Mr. Sauer said you shouldn't be out of bed, miss."

"I'm sure he did."

"I'm sensing a *but* miss?"

She smiled. "But I don't take orders from Mr. Sauer."

The man grimaced.

Tess shrugged. "I'm good here, really. No worries, Olin, okay?"

Olin didn't look convinced, but he nodded anyway. "Yes, miss." Then inclined his head and left the room.

Tess returned to her book, but after thirty minutes or so she started to get a little antsy. Propped up on crutches once again, she circled the room, not really looking for anything in particular. But when she came to an ancient-looking desk in an alcove off the main part of the library, she was intrigued. She went to the desk and sat. There were only two things on the desktop: writing paper with a modern DS embossed on the top of it, and a very nice pen. This had to be Damien's desk, Damien's chair.

She'd never been much of a snoop, but something about being at Damien's desk without him knowing made her ultracurious. She reached down and opened the long, thin drawer just under the desktop. Her pulse quickened as she searched through a few papers, a map of China and a small bag of sour candy. She didn't know what she was looking for until she found it. Two photographs. The first was of her and Damien in her college apartment, the one right off of campus. What was he doing with this, she wondered, staring at the picture.

She and Damien looked so young, and so totally happy. Why couldn't she remember that feeling?

She looked at the second photograph. How the hell had he gotten this? The photo was of her wedding day. She and Henry were standing close, holding her bouquet between them. Tess narrowed her eyes. Unlike the other picture, she didn't look exactly happy, but she did look hopeful. Things hadn't started to change yet; Henry hadn't shown his controlling side yet. Henry smiled back at her in the picture, and a shiver moved over her, settling on the scar covering her inner thigh—that hateful scar that would never go away, and would have to be explained if she ever let a man touch her below the waist.

Flashes of her early-morning makeout session with Damien went through her mind. She'd almost gotten that close with him, and he was the last person she wanted to know about her scar.

She took a deep breath and stuffed the pictures back in the drawer. Just as she closed it, she heard, "You never used to be a snoop, Tess York."

Startled, she pushed away from the desk and stood. She fumbled for her crutches.

"Need some help?" he asked.

"Nope."

He walked to her, his blue eyes glistening with mischief. "Find anything interesting?"

"Huh?"

"In my desk. When I came in you seemed fixated on something."

"Spider."

His brow lifted. "You saw a spider?"

"A big, black, hairy one," she explained, knowing full well that he not only didn't believe her, but thought her a total idiot as well. She let her head fall forward and blurted out the truth. "Okay, I was snooping and I saw the two pictures in there. I'm sorry, it was rude…"

He said nothing, and his expression was unreadable. Was he mad? Annoyed? Embarrassed? Who knew. He was giving nothing away. In fact, he changed the subject all together. "Hungry?"

"A little," she said uneasily.

"Good. I've decided that we're going to have lunch in your room."

"Okay." She actually wouldn't mind putting her foot up again. The ache had returned.

He nodded. "I'll meet you there in ten minutes. I'm going to shower first."

Tess paused, and for the first time since Damien had found her at his desk, she really looked at him. From shoes to spiky hair. He had gunk all over him, all over his hands and clothes, probably a mixture of tile adhesive and grout. Her mouth twitched as she remembered him looking like this many a time. He was a man of labor once again.

He stared at her. "What?"

"What?" she returned innocently.

"What's with the face? The grin?"

Was she grinning? That wasn't good. "You just reminded me of this guy I knew a long time ago."

"Really," Damien said in a surly tone.

She nodded. "Yep. He'd always come to pick me up with his hands and face caked with paint or something equally gross."

"Yeah, I remember that guy," Damien said, sticking his hands in his pockets. "He used to be so damn excited to see you he'd forget to clean up before driving over to your house."

"I let him use my shower, didn't I?" Tess said, grinning.

Damien's lips twitched with a faint smile. "You did more than that."

Heat rushed into Tess's cheeks, and she laughed. "Come on."

He walked toward her, his gaze eating her up. "You were damn good at getting paint off and out of the most intimate of places."

"I was a dedicated worker even then."

"I'll say." Without a warning, he scooped her up. "Too bad you've got that bandage on. I could use a little help in the shower today."

For one second she felt the urge to fight him, fight being in his arms. But the feeling quickly dissipated. She didn't have to fight him or fear him. No matter what his motives were in making her come to Tribute and fix up the house, she knew in her heart, in her gut, that Damien Sauer would never make her feel like a frightened, trapped animal.

They were nearing the door to the library when Tess called out, "Wait. My crutches."

"Nope. No crutches, no more getting out of bed."

"Fine. I'll just get Olin to swipe them for me. We're like this now." She crossed her fingers.

"Yeah, right." Damien shifted her in his arms and kept right on walking. "Come on Tess, I need you healthy and walking and back on the job."

Tess laughed as they headed down the hallway. "Manual labor getting to you already?"

"Tiling was never something I enjoyed. I liked the actual building, though." He walked into the guest room and placed her on the bed. "You might find it hard to believe, but on my jobs in California I get in there from time to time and put walls up."

"You're right. I'd find that hard to believe."

He narrowed his eyes with mock severity. "I'll be back in ten minutes."

"I can hardly wait," she said sarcastically, fighting a smile.

"I know—but you'll just have to."

For the first time in a long, long time, Tess watched a man walk away, fully enjoying the view of his lean, hard backside as he went.

The last time they'd eaten in bed, they hadn't made it past the salad.

Damien stared. And if Tess's robe crept open any further, exposing the gentle slope of her breast any more, they weren't going to make it very far today, either.

Lying on the bed, her hair loose and her face free of makeup, Tess held up her sandwich and announced, "This rivals Olivia's Croque Monsieur."

Damien grinned. "High praise?"

"The highest. This cream sauce is insane. And the ham… And these French fries," she continued, lounging back against the dense pillows. "How are they made? They're as light as a leaf."

"If you really want to know, I'll ask Marilynn."

Tess paused, stared at him, her mass of red hair falling about her face. "I can't believe you have a chef."

"Is it that you can't believe I have a chef or that I made enough money to afford one?"

She stopped eating, even put down her fry. Her eyes blazed with sincerity as she said, "I never doubted you'd be successful, Damien."

"Hmm." Why did he find that so hard to believe?

"It's true. I never thought for one second you wouldn't accomplish your goals and make a million."

"Too bad a million wasn't enough." He knew he sounded like a spoiled ass, yet he didn't attempt to apologize or take it back.

"You have the wrong idea about all of this," she said, her food forgotten as her eyes filled with melancholy. "I didn't care about money—I don't care about it now. You know my history, Damien. Losing my parents so young, and having no other family to hang on to. It was brutal. I wasn't ever looking for money. All I wanted was family, a comfortable life, a—"

"A safe life," he finished for her.

"Yes. Safe was the ultimate prize to me, it's what I felt I needed to be happy."

"I wasn't safe."

"No, you weren't. You were all about risk back then. Taking risks. And for you it paid off big-time, and I'm glad."

He didn't need her to be glad for him. He didn't want her to be glad for him. "So you made your choice based on safety."

"Yes."

"And did that make you happy? Were you happy with him?"

The expression that passed over her face was quick but very telling. Pure, unadulterated revulsion.

Damien's eyes narrowed. What the hell? What had happened when she'd left Minneapolis, when she'd left him? What had happened with the safe choice, Henry?

He was about to probe further when they were interrupted by a knock at the door.

Annoyed, he fairly shouted, "Come in."

It was Olin, looking appropriately sheepish. "Sir?"

"What is it?"

"I'm sorry, sir, but there's a problem with the house down the hill."

"What it is?"

"There's been a break-in."

"What? At one in the afternoon?"

"The workmen had gone to lunch, and when they got back the door had been knocked in."

Damien cursed. "By who?"

"A young lady," Olin supplied.

He felt Tess's gaze on him and he turned. A smile tugged at her full mouth and she lifted a brow at him. "Someone you know?"

"Doubtful," Damien said testily. "The women I know would never follow me up here and break into one of my properties."

"You sure about that?"

"Actually, Miss York," Olin said quickly, not meeting her gaze. "The woman says she's a friend of yours."

Tess looked shocked. "What?"

Olin nodded. "She was brought here. She's downstairs in the foyer. Shall I bring her up?"

Damien answered first. "Absolutely."

Eight

"You know this is insane, right?"

As she sat on the bed, in the very spot that Damien had occupied not more than sixty seconds ago, Ms. Olivia Winston's large brown eyes were filled with concern.

Tess's business partner, chef extraordinaire and, after today, nearly a class-C felon, made no bones about what was to be done. "I'm taking you home right now."

"I can't go now," Tess told her.

Olivia frowned. "Can't? Is this guy keeping you here against your—"

"No, no, no. I hurt my foot during the renovation and he's…helping me out." She wondered where Damien was now. He'd been very polite to Olivia, the woman who had broken down his door, before leaving the room.

Olivia took a deep breath and blew it out. "Jeez, Tess. When the hospital called looking for you, I completely freaked out—"

"Wait…the hospital called you?"

"Called the office. It was the number you gave on the form in the *emergency room.*" She said the last two words with real feeling.

Tess leaned back against the pillows, cocked her head to one side. "I'm sorry you got scared. It's just a cut. I had a few stitches, and I should be up and moving by tomorrow."

Olivia took a moment to process the information, then seeming somewhat pacified, she asked, "So, are you okay here—I mean, barring the foot. This guy is cool?"

"He's fine."

"Yeah, he is fine," Olivia said dryly, "gorgeous even—but is he treating you well?"

Tess laughed. "Very well. Don't worry."

"Come on, Tess. You're in a client's house, a guy who's basically a stranger. It's not right. I really think you should pack it in and come home."

Tess chewed her lip. She didn't want to go there, didn't want to tell her partner the truth. But Olivia looked as though she wasn't about to let up on the subject. "Listen, Liv, Damien Sauer isn't just a client, and he's definitely not a stranger."

Olivia's brows knit together. "Oh?"

"We used to be an item, back in my college days."

Her brows relaxed. "Oh."

"Yeah, he wanted me to renovate the house. It was the first house he bought back in the day when we were dating, and we spent a lot of time there… So I really know the ins and outs of the place."

She shrugged. "Well then, it makes sense that he'd want to hire you."

Tess gave Olivia a tight smile.

But Olivia wasn't done with the questions. "Why didn't you tell me?"

The reason was right there, on the tip of her tongue, and that's where it remained. She shook her head. "I don't know."

The three partners of No Ring Required had secrets in their past and in their present, and each had done her very best to keep those secrets hidden. But as Tess knew, and Olivia and Mary as well, eventually those secrets had a way of coming out. Maybe knowledge of that was what kept Olivia from prying and pressing Tess for more. Whatever it was, Tess was thankful.

"So," Olivia said, "do you at least want me to stay and help you finish the house?"

Tess kind of did, but she knew that Damien would never allow Olivia to stay and help her. He wanted Tess, and only Tess, to make the house into a home. She smiled at Olivia. "No. Thanks though. It's something…I have to do myself. You understand."

"Not really, but I'll take your word for it."

Tess pointed at her. "Hey, aren't you the only one at the office right now?"

"Yep."

"Well then, we need you there." Tess paused, thought of something that had the nerves in her stomach dancing. "You didn't call Mary when the hospital called you, did you?"

Olivia shook her head. "No. I thought I'd wait and see what was going on here before I interrupted her honeymoon."

"Good." Things had really changed with her partners. Five years ago they hardly spoke unless it was work related. And look at them now.

A bashful grin curved Tess's mouth as she looked at Olivia. "I can't believe you came here."

"Why?"

"We're business partners—"

Olivia leaned in and took a fry from Tess's plate. "If you say we're not friends I'm going to slap you—which would incidentally not be the greatest thing for your recovery."

Tess laughed. "No. It wouldn't."

Nibbling on the cold fry, Olivia said, "Listen, Tess, the three of us—you and Mary and I—we might've started out as 'just business partners,' but I think we're way more than that now. I think we've all been through a lot together. We've all come from something…maybe something not so great, something we want to continue to run from, but I think maybe it binds us."

Tess nodded. "Maybe."

"I believe we got together for a reason. And I hope we're friends now." She gave Tess a coy smile. "You know, I'm thinking that maybe it's not such a bad thing to have each other to lean on."

Olivia's words were passionate and truthful, and hard for Tess to ingest. Right now, anyway. Too much was happening with Damien and the ghosts of the past that he had brought with him. For now, Tess could only nod at her partner, but she hoped that Olivia would understand her small gesture, take it as a sign, a first step toward a future, a friendship.

And in Olivia's way, she did. Smiling, she pointed to Tess's plate and the Croque Monsieur. "Can I have a bite of that?"

"Of course." Tess handed her the uneaten half.

After taking a bite, Olivia sighed. "So good."

"I know, right?" Tess said, laughing.

"I can't believe you're supplying my food here. I left the office too quickly to make anything—you know how much I hate going anywhere without a food offering."

Tess nodded, said with mock seriousness, "I do. You're freakish that way."

Olivia narrowed her eyes. "Watch it, or you won't get any of the truffles I brought. I had them stashed in the freezer, so I could grab them quickly."

"You're such a sugar tease, Liv."

"So I've heard." She reached into her purse and

pulled out a square Tupperware, then she handed it to Tess. "Go nuts, Miz York."

Smiling, Tess settled back against the pillow, a Tupperware full of chocolate truffles against her chest. "So, how many clients are you juggling right now?"

"Three."

"Oh, man. You should get back."

"Not until I know you're all right."

"I'm fine."

Again Olivia narrowed her eyes. "You like being with this guy, don't you?"

Tess heard the question, but was too busy dealing with the shot of awareness that was rolling through her body to answer right away.

Olivia just sighed. "All three of us are raving lunatics when it comes to men. No common sense, no thinking things through—just allowing the beautiful man to sweep us away into a fantasy—"

"So, how is Mac, by the way?" Tess asked dryly.

"Wonderful. But he's such a guy. Did I tell you about his obsession with this portable driving range I bought him?"

"It's winter."

Olivia sighed. "He has it set up in the house. Three broken windows so far…"

For the first time since he'd been back in Minnesota, Damien felt a wave of apprehension move through him. Tess had a good friend in Olivia Winston, and he wouldn't be surprised if the dark-haired beauty had already convinced her to return to Minneapolis.

He sat at his desk in the library, staring at the photograph of Tess and Henry on their wedding day. Damien had gotten so close to finding out the truth about their marriage. The look that had crossed Tess's face. Pretty damn close to horror.

Damien gritted his teeth. Well, she deserved it, didn't she? To be unhappy in her marriage? She'd walked away from Damien for a safe, carefree life, and he was willing to bet that it had been anything but. Time would tell…

Damien thought about ripping up the picture and tossing it in the trash. He didn't need it anymore. He had her, had access to her memories, the real story. That would fuel his fire and the need for payback. But when he tried to rip the photograph in two, he couldn't do it.

"Dammit," he muttered to himself. Why did he need the thing? Was it that he had to look at them, her in that dress and him with that persuasive grin, to keep going, keep punishing her?

He sighed, thrust his hands through his hair.

Whatever the reason, he dropped the picture back in his desk and slammed it shut. Then he grabbed his coat and walked out into the hall. He heard them, Tess and her partner, laughing in the guest room. The sound filled him with lust and he forced himself to turn away and go downstairs. He wanted to be in there, in that room. He wanted to be the one who made her laugh, see her gray eyes sparkle and fill with happiness.

Olin met him at the base of the stairs.

"I'm heading over to the red house," Damien told him. "I'll be back around six."

"Yes, sir."

"If Ms. York asks…"

Olin nodded. "Yes, sir. I'll tell her."

Only for a guy who had donated millions for a new emergency room, Tess thought as she watched Tribute Memorial's chief of staff change the bandage on her foot, all from the comfort of her bed in Damien's guest room. Doctor Keith Leeds had descended on Damien's home twenty minutes ago, medical bag in hand, ready to give Tess a thorough checkup and see how she was healing.

This was an odd occurrence, to say the least, Tess thought. After all, it took a good month for her to get an appointment with her regular doctor—forget her ever-vacationing gynecologist.

"So, what do you think?" she asked him when he'd finished dressing her foot.

Dr. Leeds was short, kind and hovering around fifty. He had a full head of gray hair and liked to fiddle with his glasses when he talked. "Looks good. Really good. But more important, how does it feel?"

"Sore. But the intense pain is gone."

"I'd take things slow. No more than a few hours on it at a time."

"So, I could walk on it?"

He nodded. "Tomorrow, you should be able to get around quite well without the crutches. Just listen to your body. If the pain graduates from sore to more—"

"Nice rhyme."

He laughed. "Thank you. Sore to more, take a break, okay?"

She nodded. "Got it."

It was at that moment that Damien walked into the room. He was dressed in jeans and a black shirt and looked as though he'd just showered, his dark hair wet and spiky. Heat moved through Tess's body at the sight of him, and she turned her attention back to the doctor.

"I'll make sure she takes it easy," Damien said, holding out his hand. "Thanks for coming by, Keith. I know house calls aren't your thing."

The man shook his hand and granted him a smile. "No problem, Damien. It's on my way home."

"So, did I hear you say Tess could walk on her foot tomorrow?"

"I did."

Tess smiled broadly at Damien. "That's right, sir. Back to work."

Doctor Leeds's brow went up, and he said to Damien, "Interesting situation you have here."

Damien chuckled. "You have no idea." He walked the doctor to the door, then said, "Olin is waiting downstairs. He'll see you out."

Dr. Leeds waved at Tess. "Take care, now."

"Will do." She smiled. "Thanks again."

When he was gone, Tess settled under the covers, then proceeded to ask Damien about the new tile. "Is it all in and grouted?"

"Yes." Damien sat on the edge of the bed. "Looks good. The stone you picked out is perfect. Modern, yet warm enough for a cottage."

"Good." With large, excited eyes, she pressed a button on the remote control that was half hidden in the comforter and watched the television slowly rise out of the chest at the end of the bed. "This is the just the coolest thing." When she looked up, she caught Damien staring at her, his eyes heavy with amusement. She heaved a dramatic sigh. "Don't worry, Mr. Sauer, I'm not getting too comfortable."

"What does that mean?"

"Just because I'm fascinated with the elevator television thing doesn't mean I don't understand what happens tomorrow."

"What happens tomorrow?"

"I go back to work, and back to living in the red house."

"Back to work, maybe," he said. "For short bursts. But you're not living in that house."

"Yes, I am."

"No." He crossed his arms over his chest and waited for her to acquiesce.

She didn't. "I think it's best."

"Not for me. You've had one accident there. I'm not taking any risks with a second."

"Not taking any risks, huh?" she said slyly.

"Not with you." A wicked glint appeared in his blue eyes.

A jolt of heat flashed into her belly. Great, she thought. Twice in five minutes.

It was back—the lust—back with a vengeance. She wanted him to kiss her again, touch her, taste her.

Fear gripped her heart, went to war with the sparks of desire heating her blood. What would he think if he saw her scar, that disgusting reminder of a past they both wanted to put behind them?

But as it was, she didn't need to worry. At that moment Damien was thinking about something completely different. "If you go back to the red house and something worse happens," he was saying, "you could sue me."

He was thinking about business.

"Right." Feeling like a jerk, she turned back to the television and started flipping through the channels. "Can't have that."

They were silent for a moment. Then Damien pointed at something on the TV. "Hey, what's that?"

"What's what?"

"Go back two stations."

Curious, she did, but once there, she shook her head vehemently. "Oh, no."

"Oh, yes."

"Hey, we're not dating anymore. I don't have to pretend I like this movie."

He turned away from *Dirty Harry* and tossed her a sardonic look. "How many times did I have endure

Meg Ryan and that Barrymore girl? *French Kiss* was not about what I thought it was going to be about…"

She laughed. "Are you saying I owe you?"

"Yeah."

"You know, you could watch it in another room—you have a media room, for God's sake."

"And not see your horrified face when Clint Eastwood says that, 'Do you feel lucky? Do yah, punk?' line? What fun is that?"

"You're a sadist."

He didn't answer, just leaned over and pressed the intercom on the table by the bed.

"Yes, Miss York?"

"We need popcorn, Olin."

The man was silent for a moment, then he said quickly, "Ah, yes, sir."

Damien looked over at Tess, raised a brow. "Butter?"

She snorted. "Are you kidding? Not that much has changed in six years."

He laughed. "Extra butter, Olin."

"Very good, sir."

Damien kicked off his shoes and got in bed beside her. Not all that close, but close enough for Tess to breathe in the clean scent of his hair and skin. Close enough for her skin to tighten and feel prickly, feel desperate for his touch.

"Can you turn it up?"

She turned back to the screen and pressed the volume button. "Just so you know," she began, "*Last of the Mohicans* is on after this."

He groaned. "No way. That's not just a chick flick, that's a period chick flick."

She laughed. "After this classic here, you're gonna owe *me*."

"Fine." He reached over to press the intercom again. "But we're going to need a few beers to go with that popcorn."

He was screwed.

It was midnight, the movies were over, the beer and popcorn consumed, the room was lit by a full moon, and Damien was still in bed with Tess. She wasn't naked and sitting on top of him, but he felt as though he might explode just the same.

Halfway through the *Mohicans* movie, she'd fallen asleep, rolled in his direction and now here they were: Damien on his back and Tess curled up beside him, her arm around his waist, her head on his chest.

He was no sap, but tonight had been fun, sexy in an odd, sweet way—like old times. And he didn't want it to end. Maybe it didn't have to.

Could he just close his eyes, fall asleep and wake up with her next to him? Could he? He dropped his chin and kissed the top of her head, the soft, red curls that were scented with apples from her shampoo. He grinned. It was the same shampoo she'd used in college.

She stirred then, her knee escaping the confines of her robe and sliding up his thigh. An inch higher, he mused, and she'd feel every hard inch of him.

She moved again, her head lifting, her eyes, groggy and heavy, opening and trying to focus.

"Damien?"

He ran his thumb over her bottom lip. "Yes, sweetheart?"

"I wanted you." She spoke softly and slowly as though she was still in a dream state. Then her eyes closed again and she shook her head. "I wanted you so much."

His body went still. His fingers went under her chin and he lifted her face to his once more. "What did you say?"

Her eyes opened again and she looked like she was trying to focus.

"What did you just say, Tess?"

She licked her lips. "I want you."

Disappointment roared through him, but he dismissed the feeling. It wasn't what she'd originally said, that was for sure, but it was enough—enough to put flame to sun-dried brushwood.

He dipped his head and kissed her, gentle and slow, trying to coax a response from her. She was cautious at first, her kisses guarded and quick. But as he rubbed the back of her neck, nuzzled her lips with his own, her body relaxed and she opened for him, lapping at his tongue, matching his speed and the pressure of his mouth.

It took every ounce of self-control for Damien not to pull her on top of him and have his way with her. Every nerve ending, every muscle was alive, inside and out, and when she slid her hand up his chest, to his neck and around his head, he allowed himself to take her.

Like a possessed animal, he rolled, sending her to her back and settling himself above her. For a moment he just looked at her, watched her eyes glisten, her lips part and her chest rise and fall with every breath.

She belonged to him.

He would have to let her go soon, but for now, right now, she was his.

He bent and kissed her, her mouth, her chin, then down, his lips searing a path from her neck to her collarbone. He wanted to feel every part of her, taste every inch, make love to her until they were both too exhausted to speak about the past or even think about it.

Maybe then she'd be out of his system and he could go back to California and breathe again.

His hands moved over her collarbone and he pushed aside the white terry cloth robe, revealing her pale chest and her heavy, full breasts. She arched her back, thrusting her breasts and tight, pink nipples forward. Damien cupped them firmly, then rolled one taut nipple between his thumb and forefinger. He dipped his head and took the other into his mouth, rolled the tight peak against his tongue, lapped and suckled, then ever so gently bit down on the tip.

"Damien," she moaned, her head thrashing from side to side against the pillow, her hips thrusting, trying to meet his.

But Damien couldn't keep things slow and relaxed. He needed to be inside her body, needed to consume her. He cursed his frustration and reached down for the knot that held her robe together. But just as he'd gotten it undone, Tess put a hand over his and squeezed.

"Damien. Please. No more. I can't." She sounded like an injured bird, and Damien watched as she covered herself back up with the robe.

Like a hammer, the blood in Damien's veins pounded inside his head and chest and groin. But he wouldn't make demands or beg her to put him out of his misery. That wasn't his style.

Instead he moved off her, off the bed, stood there with his erection pressed against the zipper of his jeans.

Tess stared at the comforter. She wanted to die.

She sat there in the bright light of the round moon, not looking at Damien, not wanting to face what was coming next. She had allowed things to go too far. Again. What was wrong with her? Did she have no self-control when it came to this man?

She grabbed for the comforter and pulled it over her legs. What a fool she was. Damien had been unbelievably close to touching her scar.

"Tess?"

"Yes."

"Look at me."

Cowardice was not a part of her makeup, and she lifted her chin and looked at him. Her stomach clenched. Never had a man looked so sexy, his hair tousled, his eyes heavy, his cheeks flushed.

"What's wrong?" he asked darkly.

"This can't happen."

"It is happening."

He was right. They'd started something, and how was either of them supposed to go back? "I was half-asleep, Damien, too comfortable…"

"Don't try and pretend you didn't want this, Tess, because—"

"I'm not." She shook her head. "I did want it, but now…"

His eyes were devil-black and menacing. "And now? What?"

She stared at him, trying to think of what to say next. If she lied, was cruel, would it stop him from wanting her? Would it stop the flirtation and fun and frivolous moments?

Is that what she wanted?

No, but she couldn't have him find out her secret. And she would protect herself at all costs.

"Now I know that it's not fair to you to continue this," she said evenly.

He lifted a brow. "Oh? How so?"

She squared her jaw. "Because when I was kissing you, I was thinking about…" She stopped. She couldn't.

He looked ready to kill as he ground out, "Finish your sentence, Tess."

"No."

He stared at her for a moment, then he turned to leave.

Her heart pounded against her rib cage. This was

ridiculous, insane and juvenile. She was a grown woman, for God's sake.

His hand was on the door when she called, "Stop. Wait, Damien."

He glanced over his shoulder, said with a bored tone to his voice, "What?"

"It's not true."

He said nothing.

She continued, "It's not true." She released a breath. "I needed you to stop touching me, so I lied. You were right. So right. I loved it, every second that you were kissing me and touching me. I haven't felt that good in a long time. But I needed you to stop."

His jaw hard, he leaned back against the door. "Why?"

She shook her head. "I can't tell you."

His fist shot back, pounded the door. "Dammit! Come on, Tess. This is bull."

"Maybe. But to me it's my life."

He cursed.

"Damien, I'm going back to the red house tomorrow."

"You're not going anywhere," he said in a danger-ous voice, his gaze fierce. "And I'm warning you, don't push me on that again."

He said nothing more as he turned, gripped the door handle and threw it wide. He was gone in seconds.

Tess dropped back against he pillow, feeling mis-erable and lonely. And what made it worse was that the faint scent of him lingered on her pillow.

Nine

As the first week of renovations drew to a close, the little red house had taken on a whole new look. New windows, new tile, new tub and toilet, new cabinets and new light fixtures had been installed. Tess had worked hard with some help from Damien and of course the labor of several subcontractors.

Today the beautiful vintage floors that Tess had ordered were being put in. Normally a house was painted before the floors went down, but with her injury things had gotten a bit turned around.

After an hour or so at the red house, making sure everything was going as planned, Tess had asked Damien to drive her into Jackson to pick out the new kitchen countertops. Though her foot was much better, driving was still an issue.

They hadn't spoken a word about last night, not at the red house, not on the drive to Jackson and not as they walked through Hubbard's Tile and Stone. Tess figured it was just as well. Best to get the job done and get on with it. No entanglements, no regrets and no secrets revealed.

But then again, she missed the intimacy they'd shared last night, the fun they'd shared—and the heat of his mouth when he kissed her senseless.

As the salesman hovered at her side, Tess rubbed her hand over the honed black granite she had picked out. She sighed. "This is gorgeous." Then she pointed to the clean, white Corian. "But this is practical."

Damien finished a call on his cell phone, then stated dryly, "You know my opinion on practical."

"I do."

"Well then, you know which one to get."

Tess asked the salesman to excuse them for a moment, then she turned to Damien. "Are you like this with every project?"

"Like what?"

"Impractical. I can't see you making much money if that's the case."

His gaze turned intense and personal. "This isn't every project."

She didn't want to go there, and didn't acknowledge the look. "If you're just going to sell the place, what's the point of such personal taste?"

He lifted a brow. "Who says I'm going to sell it?" His cell rang again. He checked the number, then let the call go to voicemail.

"So, what are you going to do with it, Damien?" she asked with perhaps too much interest. "Keep it as an investment property?"

"I don't know."

"Pass it down to the next generation of Sauers?" she pressed.

He shrugged. "Perhaps. But that could be a while. I'd have to get married first."

"You don't have to get married…"

"If I'm going to make little Sauers, I do."

Tess stopped talking, stopped asking questions she didn't want the answers to. The thought of Damien having children with anyone else made her feel physically ill. Not just the act that it would take to create them, but the thought of him sharing a life, a day-to-day life with a woman and their children… she couldn't conceive of it.

Oddly enough, she'd never been able to. It was one of the things that had gotten her through the past six years, settled her with Henry—believing that Damien Sauer would never get married and have babies.

And now, here he was talking about it as though it could actually happen.

Tess turned back to the granite. "I just don't see it. You and a family. No, don't see it."

"I'm an old-fashioned guy, Tess."

"Sure." She laughed, but it was a heavy, sad sound. "The millionaire jet-setter with a glass compound and a penchant for making women pay for their mistakes."

"Just one woman," he said, his gaze intense.

"Right."

He added, "And when did you decide that leaving me was a mistake?"

She opened her mouth to deny it, then stopped, ran through what she'd just said—what had accidentally popped out. How she felt that leaving him was a mistake…

She sighed inwardly. It was a truth she hated to look at, much less admit out loud, and she pressed on, changed the subject. "Are you going to tell me what you plan to do with the house or not?"

He frowned. "I'll decide what to do with it when the work's completed."

Frustrated, she shrugged. "Fine."

"So, do you want the granite?"

"Yes, I want the granite."

Damien gestured to the salesman. "She'll take the granite." Then he walked off, his cell phone to his ear.

He couldn't sleep.

Again.

Damien glanced at the clock. Midnight. What was up with midnight? His body just couldn't seem to shut down, and his mind couldn't seem to shut off. All he could think about was her. The fact that she was down the hall, sleeping, and he wanted to be next to her again, feel the warmth of her body, her arm draped over his chest.

He rolled off the bed and threw on a T-shirt and sweats. He was a jackass, thinking he could go to her and she would welcome him into her bed as though nothing had happened, as if it was six years ago and she was waiting up for him.

But he was out his door and down the hall and knocking on her door before he could talk himself out of it.

When she didn't answer, he knocked again, even said her name. When there was still no answer, he contemplated going back to his room. But then he got a strange feeling, a worried feeling, that maybe something was wrong, and he decided to go in— deal with her ire if he had to.

He opened the door silently. It wasn't terribly dark in the room. The shades were pulled back and the moon was brilliant and nearly full, illuminating the furniture. He walked over to the bed, blinked to make sure he was seeing things clearly. Then he leaned down and flipped on the bedside lamp.

His gut clenched. The bed was made, and all of Tess's things were gone.

He muttered a curse, stalked out of the room and went to find Olin.

With a large hoop of painter's tape circling her wrist like a bracelet, Tess moved on to the next window. Tomorrow was priming and painting day, and she'd wanted to get a head start.

Well, that was mostly true.

Staying in Damien's guest room was starting to feel a little too comfortable, and kind of uncomfortable at the same time. Lying in that bed, she'd wanted him beside her, watching a movie, feeling his warmth....

She ran the tape over the window molding and snapped it off. The paint colors she chose were going to be amazing, especially with the new floors.

Oh, the floors.

They were so beautiful that when she'd gotten there tonight, she had actually sat in the middle of the living room and stared at them for a full thirty minutes. If she ever won the lottery, the beige carpet in her apartment was going into the trash and these floors were going in.

Suddenly the front door burst open and Damien stood there, looking diabolically sexy and ready to do battle.

"Holy…Jeez!" Tess gripped her chest, felt her heart slamming against her ribs.

"Get your things, we're going," Damien said, his voice low and menacing.

She glared at him. "You scared the hell out of me."

He closed the door and walked into the room, his long, wool coat trailing behind him like a villain's cape. "As if you didn't know I'd come after you."

"Well, sure I did. But I thought it would be in the morning." She was starting to believe that there was no escaping this man. "How did you even know I was gone?"

"Doesn't matter."

"Olin squealed on me, didn't he?"

Damien lifted his chin. "His loyalty should be to me."

She sighed. The poor guy. She shouldn't have put him in such an awkward position. "Don't be mad at him. I begged him to drive me, told him it was sort of a life-and-death thing."

"Whatever the reason, he made a mistake and he's fired."

Damien bent and pulled back the tarp covering the floors. Tess bent next to him, her sore foot aching a little with the movement. He looked at her. "Floors are beautiful."

Awareness moved through her, sent chills to the outside of her body and heat to the inside. Her voice was easy and intimate as she said, "You're not really going to fire him, right?"

His blue eyes softened, and he gave a small shrug. "No. But I should."

"Thanks." She sat on her backside.

Damien followed suit, looking far too handsome and put together to be sitting amongst drop cloths and paint buckets. "You don't just disappear, Tess. I told you to stay in—"

"Please, Damien," she said, putting up her hand to stop him from saying anything further. "I am not your prisoner and you are not my warden."

"This isn't about keeping you captive, Tess."

"What's it about, then?"

"Keeping you safe, dammit!"

She sighed. "That was one freak accident. It's not going to happen again."

His eyes glimmered with heat. "You're right it's not, because you're coming back with me."

"No," she said firmly.

"No?"

He looked so shocked, so vexed, she couldn't help but laugh. "I know that's hard for you to hear," she said, sobering slightly. "I'm sure you don't hear it very often."

"Tess—"

"I like this house. I feel comfortable here."

"You don't feel comfortable in my house?" he demanded darkly.

She sighed. Didn't he get it? "Damien, I can't stay there...with you."

His mouth curved into a wicked grin. "Afraid I'm going to finish what I started last night?"

"Frankly, yes."

He reached over and took her hand, then bent and kissed the inside of her wrist. "Sweetheart, it doesn't matter where we are. In that house or in this one."

"So why fight it, is that what you're saying?" The heat from his mouth had branded the skin on her wrist and she felt weak. Clearly he still remembered where her most sensitive spots were.

"Why not go with your instincts, Tess?"

She forced herself to return to reality, to remember the past and what it had taught her about instincts. "I did that once before, and it didn't turn out…it didn't turn out as I'd planned."

His brows knit together. "What are we talking about? You and Henry?"

She nodded.

"Do you want to tell me what happened?"

"You only want to know so you can use it against me."

He said nothing. Didn't agree, didn't deny it.

She pulled her hand away and shook her head. "I'm right, aren't I? There's something in you that wants to really hurt me?"

Silence met her query. Damien stared at her for a good long time before he finally said, "If I'm honest with you, will you be honest with me?"

A shot of panic went through her. How honest did he want her to be? How honest would she allow herself to be?

But even as the questions circled her mind, she looked at him and nodded.

"Yes, I want to hurt you," he said softly. "I want you to feel just a fraction of what I felt when you left. And even after we're together, after we make love—because you and I both know that's going to happen—I'll still want you to hurt because I'm an ass, a miscreant." He reached out and touched her face, his fingertips brushing gently over her cheek. "When you left, I became someone else, a machine, a man with no soul."

His words cut deeply into her, fisted around her heart. Six years ago she left the man she loved for a promise of what she'd always believed would make her happy. The mistake had cost her in so many ways.

It was her turn, and he was waiting. She knew she wouldn't go all the way with the truth, but Damien deserved to hear as much as she could give him. "My marriage was a lie." She saw the surprise register on his face, but just kept going. "I wanted the perfect little life, the perfect family. Henry promised me that, and I believed him. When we knew each other in college, he was uncomplicated and sweet, but one week after we got married he showed me who he really was."

"And who was that?" Damien asked softly.

She swallowed the knot in her throat. "A mean, manipulative, controlling monster."

Damien said nothing, just stared at her, expressionless.

She said shakily, "You think I got what I deserved, right?"

He stood, held out his hand for her. "Come on, Tess."

"Henry took away my faith and my hope." She felt so tired all of a sudden. She put her hand in Damien's and let him pull her to her feet.

"You think I deserved it…" she started weakly.

But Damien was clearly done with the conversation. "Get your things," he said. "We're going back to the house."

* * *

Damien sat on a stool at the minidiner inside Wanda's store. It was hours past closing time, but when he'd shown up on Wanda's doorstep a few minutes ago, she hadn't turned him away.

With wild graying hair and a robe so thick it could double as a winter coat, Wanda poured them each a cup of coffee, then took the seat beside him at the Christmas-festooned counter. "Well, well, well…"

"I know. It's late."

"Never mind that," she said. "Are you going to tell me what the problem is or do I have to guess?"

The problem. He wasn't exactly sure himself. He just knew that after dropping Tess off at the house and getting her settled—then tossing out some threats to Olin regarding the penalties given if he ever offered Tess a ride to the red house in the middle of the night again—he'd needed to get out of his house.

Wanda grunted at him. "Fine. I'll guess. Business?"

"No."

"Must be personal, then. Not my favorite thing to discuss, but I'll do it. Spill."

The cat clock above the griddle meowed twice. Two o'clock in the morning. Damien shoved his hands through his hair. "You know how I got so successful, Wanda?"

She grinned at him. "Fine brain, fine man."

He chuckled halfheartedly. "No. Try follow through and a killer instinct."

"My second guess."

"I made a plan and I followed it through to the letter. No second thoughts, no kindness, no compassion."

"And?"

"And I'm having second thoughts about my plan."

She stood, reached over the counter and grabbed a small bottle. "Why?"

"I don't know." But he did, actually. After hearing Tess's confession about her bogus marriage and Henry being a monster, he was having second thoughts about his plans to hurt her. If she'd been hurt already, how could he...

"Come on, Damien," Wanda said, pouring the liquid from the small bottle into each mug of coffee, which, knowing Wanda, was probably whiskey. "You just don't want to admit the reason because it'll make you feel like less of a man."

Damien grinned at her over his hootch-laced coffee cup. She never let him get away with anything. He'd been parentless for more than fifteen years now, and had done just fine on his own. Then he'd met Wanda, and she'd offered her friendship and sage advice and over the years had become a motherly figure to him.

"It's the woman you met—the redhead," he admitted darkly.

Wanda nodded. "Thought so. But, Damien, hon, you can't let love influence your decisions."

"You're the only woman I know who'd say that."

Wanda just smiled and sipped her coffee.

"And incidentally," he added, "this isn't about love."

"No?"

"No." Then he amended the statement. "Well, not love now. There was love in the past and it was thrown back in my face, and you know how well a man takes something like that."

"I do. So use it. Use the anger and pain and stomped-on pride. Use that to regain your momentum and stop those second thoughts."

"Why aren't you trying to talk me out of my plan and into the flowery world of forgiveness?"

Wanda poured the rest of whatever alcohol had been in the bottle into her empty coffee cup. "Hell, Damien, if I advise you to forgive and move on, then I've got to do it myself."

"Who are you talking about?" Wanda had been seeing her produce supplier for a few months now. Damien didn't know the guy all that well. But he did know the man's name. "Is it Paulo? Did you two have a fight, because I will break him in two if he hurts you—"

"No, no." She shook her head. "This is way before Paulo."

"Well, who was it then?"

"You don't know him, my first husband—"

"You were married before?"

"That's enough now. My past is my own and I don't like 'sharing time.'" She drained her cup, then stood. "I need my beauty sleep and you need to get back to your life." She leaned in and kissed him on the cheek. "Lock up when you go, all right?"

"Sure."

Damien drank the rest of his coffee, but didn't move from the counter. Wanda was right. Every time he felt connected to Tess, felt sorry for her, he needed to go back in time and remember how she'd walked away without giving a damn about how he felt.

He needed to revise his plan. He needed to remember that he hadn't come back to Minnesota to rekindle a romance, but to get close to Tess again, make her love him, then make her pay.

And as soon as her foot had totally healed, that's just what he was going to do.

Ten

Stitches out and foot feeling good.

Tess walked out of the doctor's office, sans crutches and Band-Aid free. The doctor, who, even after Tess had assured him that it had been no trouble getting there, had insisted that he could've come to Damien's house for the final checkup.

But Tess wasn't an invalid anymore and she didn't want to act like one. She could walk and work and drive again. And Damien, thank goodness, hadn't given her any trouble, even when she'd told him that she was going to take a cab to the doctor's office and not his town car.

In fact, Tess mused as she walked out of the building and down the sidewalk toward the waiting cab, Damien hadn't made any trouble or made any passes at her in the past few days.

After coming home from painting the red house, he'd basically checked in on her, then disappeared. Could the reason stem from all those things she'd told him about Henry and her marriage?

As she sat in the back of the taxi, she wondered if Damien had given up on her, didn't want to deal with her baggage and had his sights set on someone else. The thought of him even looking at another woman made her lungs feel as though they were having the air squeezed out of them.

When her cab pulled into the driveway of the little red house, the first thing Tess saw was Damien, looking very sexy under the December sun. He had shoveled the snow off of a large patch of grass and had put down a tarp. On top of the tarp were the kitchen cabinets. Damien had work clothes on, and he didn't look up when she got out of the car.

Not until she was practically upon him.

"Hey," she called as she walked toward him.

He glanced up, over his shoulder. "Hey, there." Even with the slight warmth of the sun, the cold, clear morning had brought color to his cheeks, and his blue eyes glittered like sapphires.

"What are you doing?" she asked him.

"Sanding the cabinets."

"They look good."

"They're a work in progress."

"Well, I just came from the doctor and he said I'm good to go."

"What does that mean?" he asked.

"That means you don't have to do this anymore. Go home, get back to your regular life, and I'll take over here."

He paused, thought about this, then said, "I don't think so."

"Excuse me?"

He stood, looked down at her with a resolute expression. "I've decided that we're going to finish this house together."

Her heart started to pump faster. "You have?"

"Yes."

"Why?"

"Could be fun."

"Yeah, but doesn't that defeat the purpose?"

He cocked his head. "What purpose is that?"

"Making me suffer, making me work my backside off as punishment for my sins."

A wicked smile tugged at his lips. "I think your backside is pretty perfect the way it is."

Heat swirled in her belly and her legs felt shaky and weak. She tried not to smile too broadly.

"The truth is," he began evenly. "I need to get back to California sooner than I expected."

"Oh." She tried to mask the disappointment she felt, but she wasn't sure if she'd pulled it off.

"I need everything done by Wednesday."

Her jaw dropped. "That's two days away."

"That's right."

He seemed so blasé about the whole thing, but Tess just wasn't up for pretending she was, too. "I'd better get on the phone and see if we can have the countertops and furniture delivered ASAP."

As she walked toward the house, Damien called after her. "Throw money at the problem. That always works for me."

Tess didn't get it. Who was this guy? This chameleon? Warm and vulnerable one moment, then cold and demanding the next.

She went inside and took out her cell phone, dialed the number for Hubbard's Tile and Stone. As she spoke with the manager about changing their delivery date, she tried not to think about how in just two days Damien would be out of her life for good.

It had been a long, dusty day, but much had been accomplished. The cabinets were sanded, stained and affixed to the newly painted kitchen walls. The bathroom was completely done, the bedroom, too. The only things that needed to be done were the countertops, moldings, outlet covers, a few fixtures and the furniture. Tess had already brought back the three pieces she'd bought from Mr. Opp, and the other two delivery companies had jumped at the extra cash, and were going to be at the red house tomorrow before noon.

Tess stood in the living room and sighed. She hadn't expected to fall in love with the house all over again. It had always been cute, but now it was modern and charming. It was how she would redo her home if she had the funds. It was perfect, and no doubt some perfect little family would stumble upon it and make it theirs.

Just moments ago Damien had gone out for pizza, and Tess decided to get cleaned up and get off her feet at the same time. She headed into the bathroom. The soapstone spa tub she'd picked out looked inviting. Would it be so wrong if she tried it out?

She sat on the edge of the tub and turned the knobs. Water gushed from the tap. Hot, steamy water. Just the sight of it made her muscles relax.

Ten minutes later, she was up to her neck in bubbles, daydreaming about a man with dark hair and blue eyes, who was hovering over her, ready to explore every inch of her body. Just as she was about to let him, there was a knock on the bathroom door.

"Tess?"

Damien's booming voice brought her instantly back to reality and she sat up, sloshing water over the sides of the tub. "Yes. What?"

"You okay in there?"

"Yeah. Of course. Just cleaning up."

"In the new bathtub?" She heard the amusement in his voice.

"I had to make sure it was…"

"Seaworthy?" he supplied.

"Comfortable."

"I have the pizza, and I got those garlic knots you like."

She smiled at the thoughtfulness of his gesture. She called out, "You can go ahead and eat if you want."

"No, I'll wait. Take your time."

Yeah, as if she could just lie back and relax with him out there waiting for her. Not possible.

"I'm done," she called, standing and stepping out of the water. But in her rush, she knocked the bar of soap she'd just used off the holder and onto the floor. It made a loud thud of a sound. She called out a rather terse, "Dammit," as she leaned over to retrieve it.

She knew her mistake the minute she stood up again.

She heard his footsteps, then the door opened before she could even grab a towel. Her heart slammed against her ribs and a silent scream escaped her throat as she realized that he was going to see— her leg. The scar on her leg.

No, no. She couldn't let him.

But it was too late. He was coming through the door. "What was that? Are you okay?"

"Damien get out!" she shouted, full on panic in her tone. "Out. Please."

But like anyone with a disaster in their sites, Damien couldn't look away. "Tess?"

She felt weightless, out of her body.

He cocked his head to one side and his eyes narrowed, he stared at her inner thigh, at the massive burn scar that had eaten up her smooth, beautiful skin five years ago. "What the hell happened to you?"

Misery gripped her and she shook her head. "Please go."

His gaze found hers. "Was that an accident?"

"No. Now please go."

"Someone did this to you? He looked horrified. "Who—" He took a few steps closer. "Holy sh—"

"Damien, please don't." She grabbed the towel off the hook and wrapped it around herself.

"Why didn't you tell me?" he demanded, going to her, pulling her into his arms. "Oh, my God, why didn't you come to me?"

She shook her head. "I couldn't."

"You could have."

Her towel slipped, and she tried to retrieve it, but Damien stopped her.

Her eyes implored him. "I need it."

"Screw the towel." He looked into her eyes, his own so stormy, so intense and she saw the man, the boy from long ago. And he was thoroughly pissed off. "I'm going to kill him."

"Too late."

He wrapped his arms around her and held her close, kissed her hair, her neck, her mouth. Against her lips, he uttered miserably, "You should've come to me."

Wearing nothing, the air hitting her scar, she felt so vulnerable. "And what would you have done, Damien? Tell me I deserved it?"

He tipped her face so she could see him, see the passion in his eyes. "Never, do you hear me? Never." Before she could respond, he slipped an arm under her legs and lifted her up, then he headed out of the bathroom.

She wrapped her arms around his neck. "Where are you taking me?"

"Somewhere where I can kiss you properly," he said, leaving the bathroom.

"You *were* kissing me."

He paused at the bedroom door, his gaze moving over her mouth. "I need you on your back for this kind of kissing."

Excitement warred with the panic in her belly. She'd dreamed about him touching her, kissing her, spreading her legs apart and using his tongue to drive her mad. But in every fantasy, her leg was unblemished, smooth and perfect.

She didn't want him to see her, touch that part of her….

He placed her on the bed and bent his head, applying soft, teasing kisses over her toes, then little nibbles at her ankles. Up he went, suckling her calves and the soft spot over her knee. Tess wanted to enjoy it, but she couldn't allow herself to let go. He was so close to seeing it, feeling— So close to her scar.

"No, Damien, please." She put her hand over the rough skin on her inner thigh.

"Sweetheart, let me touch you, please." His warm hand moved up her leg, gently forcing her hand off her scar.

Tess could barely breathe. "I'm not…can't…it's ugly…"

"No, sweetheart. You're beautiful."

And then he was there, applying soft kisses to the rough, sensitive surface of her scar, and Tess loved it and hated it at the same time. While her mind roared with thoughts and fears from her past, Damien kept talking to her, whispering sweet, erotic words as he soothed her with his hands.

So many nights she had dreamed of this, wondered if she'd ever feel sexual, if she'd feel desired by a man. On a hungry groan, Damien moved upward to the wet curls between her legs. She could feel his breath on her, and she released a tense, excited sigh.

"My Tess," he uttered as he reached beneath her and cupped her buttocks, squeezed the round flesh until she lifted her hips. Then he lowered his head.

Tess stared at him, at his head between her legs, electric heat flickering inside of her at the erotic sight.

And then he touched her with his tongue, soft, slow circles over the hard bud that she'd thought for so long was dead.

"Damien, please…" She didn't know what she was asking for.

But Damien responded to the ache of desperation in her voice by nuzzling her, lapping at the tender bud with his deliciously rough tongue, suckling it deep until she wriggled beneath him, called his name again.

Tess pumped her hips, feeling as though she could cry, it felt so good. She wanted the incredible heat and pressure to last forever.

As she fisted the white comforter, pointed her toes and mewled like animal in pain, Damien's mouth teased and twisted. Beads of sweat broke out on her forehead as his hands gripped her buttocks. No matter how desperately she wanted to, Tess couldn't hold on to the sweet feeling for much longer.

It had been so long, and the pressure was building and had to be released. And then she called out, thrust her hands in his hair and spread her legs as wide as she could.

Damien gave a guttural sound of approval, then sank his tongue deeply inside her. Blinding heat surged through her as she shook with climax. Her body was out of control and on fire and she pressed against his mouth, taking his tongue into her body, then out again. Over and over until the pressure eased, then subsided.

When it did, Damien sat up. His gaze was thunderstorm dark, and he looked ready to pounce. Quick as a jungle cat, he pulled off his clothes, grabbed a condom from his pocket then sheathed himself.

Unable to breathe, to think clearly, Tess watched every move he made, watched his hand glide over his thick, hard erection, watched the muscles in his chest and abdomen tighten when he did.

The muscles between her legs quivered with anticipation. She remembered how well their bodies fit together, and the wait was torture. She'd waited too long. They both had. She wanted him on top of her, his shaft inside of her.

When Damien was poised above her, the long, hard length of him bobbing sensually against her belly, she licked her lips. She had been starved for so long.

Not anymore.

Her legs were weak and shaky, but her body craved more and she opened for him, no longer self-conscious about her scar. The slick evidence of her need dripped from the center of her onto the bed sheets, and as Damien watched, his eyes glittering with need, he reached out and touched her, played with the damp curls above until he found the wet folds beneath. Tess's breath caught in her throat as his fingertip circled the entrance to her body with slow, torturous strokes.

Panting and dizzy, Tess let her head fall to one side as she pressed herself into his hand. "Damien, please. I want you."

Damien was over her in seconds, the hard tip of his erection poised at the entrance to her body. And then he entered her, slowly, one delicious inch at a time, stretching her, giving her body what it craved, what it remembered.

When he was all the way inside of her, he hovered there, his gaze locked to hers. "Hey."

Her arms went around him and she smiled. "Hey."

As she stared up into his eyes, their breath mingling, their bodies joined, she knew she had fallen in love with him. Or was it *back* in love with him?

Maybe she had never stopped.

The heat inside of her continued to build, demanding that she take it and release it. She wrapped her legs around his waist, and he starting moving, slowly pumping inside of her until she caught his rhythm, the perfect rhythm. Her hands drifted down his back and over his buttocks. She loved the way his muscles flexed as he thrust deeper and deeper inside of her.

Damien bent his head and kissed her, nuzzled at the entrance to her mouth until she opened for him. His tongue lapped at hers, mimicking the movement of their bodies.

Tess was growing restless again as the building pressure of orgasm was upon her. Heat and pleasure swirled through her, and when Damien slipped his hand between them and spread her wide, pressed himself against her and rode her hard, she felt her mind slipping away and the slow, booming fire of climax returning, taking over every muscle, every limb, every inch of her hot skin.

Damien must have felt it, too, because his thrusts turned from tame to wild, his forehead glistened with sweat and he reached underneath her buttocks and lifted her higher.

His erection slammed against the sweet spot inside of her, the core of nerves that had only ever been turned on by this man.

"Oh, yes, Damien," she called, thrusting her hips upward in a wild, jerky motion as he thrust into her. Her skin was slick, hot and she ached for release. Damien gave it to her with one hard thrust against that soft, aching spot deep within her and she cried out, gripping his back, thrusting her hips.

Damien shuddered, his body racked with the spasms of climax. Saying her name over and over, he lifted up and plunged back down, burying himself as deep as he could go. Then his body gave one last tremor and he collapsed on top of her.

Tess held him close, breathing heavily, her eyes closed tightly as she felt small aftershocks of her release play through her. Feeling so close to Damien, Tess stroked his back and buttocks, even lifted her hips to feel him deep inside of her again as their bodies cooled.

After a few minutes Damien tried to roll to one side, but she held him there.

"I'm going to smother you," he said softly, gently.

She shook her head and held tight. "No, I love it."

This man's weight on her was pure heaven and she just wanted to feel him for as long as she could have him. But after a few minutes his prediction was correct and her chest started to grow weary from the pressure.

She let him roll to his back, and smiled when he took her with him. He held her possessively, curled her against him, and as they started to breath normally again, he played with her long red hair, his fingers dancing in her curls.

"Damien?"

"Hmm?"

"There's something I have to say."

He paused, then said softly, "Okay."

She closed her eyes, snuggled deep into his arm. "Back then, six years ago, when we were together, I had so much passion for you, so much love. I thought that such a deep love, such an intense attraction couldn't last. Honestly, I thought a real, committed relationship, the kind that went on for fifty years, had to be something tamer and more sensible."

"Oh, Tess. That's silly."

"I know. I was an idiot."

"You were young."

"Yes, I was a young idiot."

He chuckled softly. "Doesn't matter."

"Sure it does."

"No, sweetheart. All that matters is what you believe now."

She'd never felt so safe, so happy. She knew the feeling was probably a temporary one, but she didn't care. She was going to enjoy it for as long as possible.

She ran a hand over his chest, played in the sprinkling of damp hair. "I believe that love is the most important gift. I believe in second chances and that being afraid of your feelings can only lead you down the path of unhappiness and regret. And I'm done with regret."

Damien pulled her even closer and kissed her hair.

Tess nuzzled his chest. "You know, I was leaving him when he got in the accident. It was the day after he gave me the scar. He was following me. He swore he'd always follow me. That's when he got into the car accident."

"Oh, Tess." Damien kissed her hair softly. "Don't think about it. It's done."

She rose up on her elbow and looked at him, deep into the dark-blue fire of his eyes. "What about us, Damien? Are we done?"

Damien's eyes turned hungry and his jaw clenched, but before he could say anything, Tess put her fingers over his mouth, his full sexy mouth, which just minutes ago had made her body ache with pleasure. "Don't answer that. Not tonight, not now."

On a growl he pulled her to him and kissed her hungrily.

"Stay here with me," she whispered against his mouth. "Don't go back to the house tonight."

He nipped at her bottom lip, uttered hoarsely, "I'm not going anywhere."

She smiled, then dropped her head back down and snuggled into the crook of his arm. "We'll work together, be together…for now."

He held her tightly and she closed her eyes, let her heart relax and her heartbeat slow, until finally she gave in to sleep.

It was close to dawn when Tess climbed on top of Damien and eased herself down on his thick, hard, shaft. Outside the bedroom window, snow fell to the ground, blanketing the earth, the glistening white color illuminating the walls of the room and the naked skin of the two people making love in it.

His back to the warm sheets, Damien stared up at her. His body rigid with need, he watched her eyes dance with hunger, her breasts rise and fall and her hips sway back and forth. He had been here a hundred times in his mind, had planned this moment, but nothing could compare with the reality.

She brought her legs forward, bracketing his shoulders, and settled her hands back on his thighs, giving Damien perfect access to her swollen cleft. As he watched her move his erection in and out of her body, the perfect connection that he would die before breaking, he placed his thumbs on either side of her wet folds. Gently, he opened her and began to circle the tender bud.

Tess sucked air between her teeth and dropped her head back, moaning with pleasure. The light played off her skin, turned her hard nipples into a ghostly pink and the scar on her thigh to a blatant reminder of a horrible past she wanted so desperately to leave behind and never revisit.

And he was planning on hurting her again....

He was a monster.

Her thrusts quickened and Damien's mind turned off. She was close, so close, and as he flicked the sensitive, white-hot bud back and forth, over and over, she let go, arched her back and called out.

The sound and the heat were too much for Damien. As she pumped and moaned, her muscles fisting around his erection, he finally allowed himself to go, fly, follow her over the edge into the sweet ecstasy of climax.

Eleven

It was nearly nine in the morning. Damien and Tess stood in the newly remodeled kitchen, wearing next to nothing. As they waited for the coffeepot to do its thing, they jovially debated some of Tess's choices in her purchases for the home.

Grinning, Tess wrapped her arms around Damien's neck and tried to help him remember their initial deal regarding the furniture-buying decisions. "I seem to recall you saying—many times, in fact—that I should consider this my house when I do the design."

His hands went around her waist. "That was before I saw the pot rack."

"What's wrong with the pot rack?" she asked,

mystified. "It's stainless steel. Who doesn't like stainless steel?"

"I hit my head on it this morning when I was getting a glass of water."

She laughed. "You are very tall."

"Hey, you're supposed to be sympathetic."

"I am?"

"You're my wife, after all."

"Wife for hire," she corrected.

He shrugged. "Technicality."

Her heart tugged at his words, and she rolled onto her toes and gave him a quick kiss. "I can have the pot rack taken up—"

"You mean taken down?"

"No," she said, giving hive a playful swat.

"And then there's the sink."

She turned her head and stared at the white porcelain farm sink. "What's wrong with the sink?"

"It's a bathtub."

"It's beautiful."

"You could get two kids in here!"

"Well, maybe I'll have two kids, then," she teased.

But the teasing part was lost on Damien. His smile died instantly, and a cloud moved over the brightness of his eyes.

"I just meant someday," she said lightly, noting the stiffness in his arms as he held her. "Someday I'll have a sink of my own like this, and maybe someday I'll have a couple kids to stick in it."

Not much better, Tess.

Damien's blue eyes narrowed. "Who are you planning on having kids with?"

She didn't know what to say. "I don't know. I was just playing—"

"Yeah." He released her, walked over to the sink. "I don't like it."

Neither did she. She didn't want to think about him being with someone else either or having kids…. But this was their last full day together and he hadn't given her any indication that he wanted the relationship to continue after he went back to California tomorrow.

"Coffee's ready," she said, trying to force a light tone into her voice. "Counters should be here in a few hours." She glanced around. "This place is so great, so fresh. You know, you could rent it out if you wanted to. Hang on to the property, if you wanted to. Someone might like it for a getaway. Tribute's got that cute, charming, small-town feel."

"We'll see," he grumbled, his dark, irritated gaze raking over her.

"Why are you looking at me like that?"

"I can't get the thought of you and another guy and kids out of my head."

Sighing, she put her arms around him and pressed herself against him. "You know what? I'm a little tired from last night. How about you?"

"No."

She smiled to herself. "I think you are. I think you could do with a nap."

When she glanced up, his eyes were changing from frustrated to ferocious as he got her meaning. With a hungry growl, he lifted her up and held her in his arms possessively. "I'm taking you to bed."

"Good."

His brow lifted wickedly. "But just so we're clear, there'll be no napping going on."

By the time the sun went down that day, the house was complete. From soup to nuts. And Tess had never felt so proud yet so cheerless in her life. Not that she was going to let Damien see how sad she was. In fact, she had planned a lovely night for them. Dinner by the fire, then a repeat performance of that morning.

Tess heard the shower running as she put the water on the stove to boil. In her mind's eye, she could see Damien, naked and wet, the water sluicing over his skin.

One thing was certain, a night or two of sleeping with him, making love with him, wasn't going to be enough, and she imagined that after he left for California her life would return to that empty shell it had once been.

She turned into the cutting board and set to work chopping tomatoes for sauce. She wished she knew how Damien felt. But he didn't give her much. Sure, he didn't want to think of her with another man or having another life, but he'd been tight-lipped about the future and what he wanted.

Was it possible that he might want to continue seeing her? Long distance? Or maybe moving to Minnesota part-time?

She stopped chopping. One thing she did know for certain was that being here together, in Tribute, had changed them both. And the red house represented that change. From something that was broken-down, messed up and battle-scarred, the little red house had been transformed into a clean, warm, safe, happy place. And Tess and Damien had been transformed along with it.

Tess turned off the burner and left the kitchen. She needed to see Damien, feel him, feel his arms around her again.

The shower was still running, and as she entered the bathroom, she was engulfed in hot, wet steam. Her heart pounding with need, Tess stripped off her clothes, then pulled back the shower curtain.

Damien looked even better than she could possibly imagine, every inch of his hard, muscled body dripping with water.

He grinned at her and offered his hand. "Dirty mind or just plain dirty?"

She took his hand and stepped inside. "A little of both."

"Good answer," he said, turning her so her back was to his front. He pulled her against him, against his already-hard shaft, then took the soap in his hand and began to wash her. Down her neck and over her collarbone.

"You let me know when you're clean," he whispered in her ear.

She smiled.

He moved the slippery bar over her breasts, over each tight, hard nipple. "How about now?"

She shook her head and uttered a shaky, "No."

He slipped the soap over her stomach, down over her hip bones, then between the wet curls at her core. "Here? Is this where you need my help?"

She nodded, unable to speak as he stroked her with the slippery soap, as he washed away the feelings of sadness and uncertainty, as he sent her to the moon again and again…

The phrase *eating in bed* had taken on a whole new meaning for Damien tonight. Like the perfect wife, Tess had served him spaghetti and champagne, pausing every so often to kiss him, nuzzle him and tell him she couldn't stop thinking about what he had done to her in the shower.

It was pure hell.

And total heaven.

He was leaving for California tomorrow night and everything inside of him was screaming to stay, to forgive her, let it go and try to be happy for once in his miserable life. But there was a force stronger than his feelings for Tess at work here, something that had been six years in the making, an undeniable force.

Damien downed his glass of champagne, then

turned to look at Tess. He had never seen her look more beautiful. Happiness and the glow of great sex radiated on her face.

The sucker, the fool inside of him could only think how great it would be to see her look like that every day, every morning when he opened his eyes.

He inhaled deeply, trying to quell the sudden feeling of being pissed off. "Hey, Tess, can I ask you something."

"Sure."

"Do you have any regrets?"

She laughed. "Tons."

"No, I mean, about coming here."

"I didn't have much choice, if you recall." She smiled over her glass of champagne. "But no, I'm glad I came here." She shrugged. "Maybe this started out as payback for you, maybe it still is, but whether you like it or not it's ending up being the best thing that could ever happen to me."

His brow creased. "How's that?"

She looked up for a moment. "I feel free, for the first time in six years…even longer, maybe."

He stared at her. Dammit! He had a plan in motion already, an anvil poised and ready to crush the dreams they'd built over the past two weeks. But what? She had made her peace with him already, with being here? She'd found freedom by being here and he was responsible for that?

What the hell? Did she deserve to feel free after what she'd put him through? And did he still have a right to want to make her pay? After everything he knew and had seen.

He didn't know. But as she put her glass down and slid the sheet off of his body, as she kissed his ear, then his neck and his chest, he decided he didn't need an answer tonight.

What he did need was her, her heart, her eyes locked with his as she scattered kisses over his chest, down his belly, down to where he ached for her with granitelike hardness….

Twelve

Tess woke to bright sunshine streaming through the bedroom window, and a Damien-less bed. At first, she panicked, thinking he had already left for California, but as she read the note on his pillow, her tension eased.

He had a meeting, and he'd be back by one.

Five hours…what could she do? The house was done, furniture in, appliances up and running. Sure she could pack, but what fun was that?

Then an idea popped into her head. A Christmas gift for Damien. The perfect gift.

With her pulse pounding, she jumped out of bed and headed into the bathroom. She just hoped she could find someone with enough skill to make it, to create the perfect representation of what had happened here in this house, between the two of them.

She knew that trying to find that perfect gift in such a short amount of time was a long shot, but it was something she had to do.

It was just business.

He would tell himself that until the day he died.

Damien pulled his sleek, black car into the driveway and shut off the engine. Before he got out, he stared at the little red house, testing himself. Did the place evoke any feelings that were useless to him now? Warmth, caring, vulnerability, comfort?

Of course they did, and Damien instantly hardened himself.

From day one, his plan had been to make Tess love him, make Tess love the house, then sell it without a thought. He had been a cold bastard then. And over the past two weeks, he had surprised himself by allowing Tess to get under his skin and melt his icy heart.

But the truth remained; she had hurt him once, screwed him over big-time. What guarantee did he have that she wouldn't do it again?

Better to cut things off here, cut her loose, and if it had to be in a blatantly obvious and hurtful way, so be it.

He stepped out of the car into the freezing air and walked to the front door. The offer that had just been made to him was highly lucrative, and needed to be acted on immediately.

When he came through the door, everything that was Tess cried out to him. The happy fire in the fireplace; the peaceful furniture in the living room; the quiet, sensual paint colors on the wall; and that damn sink in the kitchen.

Then he heard her. She was in the bedroom, talking on the phone in a merry voice. He stepped into the doorway and lifted his chin in a silent hello.

Sitting cross-legged on the bed, her hair loose about her shoulders, Tess caught sight of him and waved. Her gray eyes were bright, and she was clearly happy to see him.

"No, the foot is fine," she was saying to whoever was on the other end of the line. "I'm so much better, Liv. All healed." She looked up at Damien then, a smile tugging at her perfect mouth. "He's been wonderful." Her smile widened and she winked. "I do. Even more. Honestly, I've never felt this way before."

Damien's gut twisted as he realized what she was saying. She loved him.

Damn her. She loved him. Now. And she had said it out loud, to his face.

She'd never felt this way before.

Anger bubbled inside of Damien and he walked out of the room. He went into the living room and stood by the fire. He *had* felt this way before and look where that had gotten him.

It played like a broken record in his head. He had loved her and she had walked out on him, and even though he'd tried to bury it these past few weeks, those wounds were still fresh.

Maybe selling the house, tearing this little world to bits right in front of her would help heal him—maybe not.

But it was done, the deal was done.

He heard her walk up behind him, felt her hand on the small of his back. "That was Olivia."

"I guessed."

Her arms went around him. "How was your meeting?"

"Fruitful." Unlike the crackling fire beside him, Damien's voice lacked warmth, and was completely emotionless.

"Well, that's good," she said, sounding a little confused by his tone. "Was it about a house?"

"Yes, this one."

"Oh." And that's all it took. She released him.

He turned to face her. It killed him to see the disappointment and worry in her gray eyes, but there was nothing for it. "There was an offer made on it."

Her brows went up. "Wow. Without even seeing the place?"

"They didn't need to see it."

"Seriously, with all the work we've done. That sounds odd."

"They don't care about the renovations," he said, being careful to keep his voice casual.

"Then they're idiots because—"

"Tess." He stopped her right there. "They don't want the house."

Her eyes narrowed and she shook her head. "I'm sorry, you've lost me."

"They want the land."

"Well, the house is on the land, so—"

"They want to build a motel here, and they've offered me a considerable amount of money."

The doubtful, sad look she'd worn just moments ago was now replaced with the glare of a woman who understood what it was like to be hurt and was ready for it to happen again. "They have to tear down the house to do that, don't they?"

He nodded. "Yes."

She released a weighty breath and crossed her arms over her chest. "So what did you tell them?"

"I told them nothing," Damien said evenly. "I asked them where I should sign."

Tess stared at him. She felt numb, except for the scar on her inner thigh. For some reason, the skin there burned like the devil.

Maybe because she was dealing with the devil.

She left Damien standing beside the fire and walked to the couch to sit. She felt like the world's biggest fool. Her happy mood, her trusting spirit—the gift she'd spent hours designing for him. But mostly, for even thinking that there might be a future for them.

Clearly, it wasn't in the cards, never had been.

His back to the fire, Damien attempted to explain. "It's business. A great deal."

"I'm sure it is."

"And I know you worked hard on the property, so there will be a substantial compensation—"

"I don't want your money, Damien," she said, her gaze and tone reflecting the insulting offer he'd just made.

But Damien didn't get it. "Why the hell not? You could use it for your business or—"

"Or nothing," she uttered, disgusted.

But, for whatever reason, he wouldn't let up. "Take the money, Tess."

She stood and stalked over to him, faced him with her jaw tight and her lower lip quivering. "What is wrong with you?"

His blue eyes were almost lifeless in their apathy. "What do you mean?"

"A few hours ago you were nuzzling my neck."

"Things change," he said coldly.

"What exactly changed for you?" She lifted her brows. "Come on, I can take it. I'm no schoolgirl anymore, as we both know."

His gaze dropped and he turned to the door. "I have to get back to the house. But you should be aware that the bulldozers are coming tomorrow. Eight a.m."

"What?" she called after him.

"Eight a.m." he repeated, then walked outside.

She followed him out, into the cold afternoon air. "I heard the time part, Damien."

"They wanted to move fast, Tess."

She watched him walk away as her socks grew damp from the snow on the walkway. Then it finally dawned on her. Stupid, silly Tess, who had allowed herself to be whisked off into a fairy tale, minus the happily-ever-after part.

Tearing down the house had been his goal from day one. Have her build her dream, her perfect family home, then tear it down—while tearing the girl who'd hurt him to shreds in the process.

Damien was nearly at his car when she shouted, "Stop right there!"

He did, then turned and stared coldly at her as she walked toward him. "You're going to freeze. Go back inside."

She was in his face, feeling nothing but a burning desire to punch him. "You knew from the beginning that there was a good possibility that this house was going to be torn down, didn't you?"

"There were many possibilities."

"And you had me picking out the most beautiful materials…" She shook her head. "My fantasy materials."

He leaned against the open door. "I wanted you to feel what it was like to have something you loved ripped from you."

She just stared at him, not believing what she was hearing. "Oh, Damien. You really think I'd be emotionally destroyed because this house is gone?"

He didn't answer, but his jaw went hard as steel.

"You don't get it, do you?" she said, her warm breath making small clouds in the cold afternoon air.

"Get what?" he muttered.

"What the true payback is. You did hurt me, Damien. Make no mistake about that—you succeeded there. The true payback is that I actually thought we had something…real. I thought we'd both grown up enough to get over the past and start something that was so amazing." Her throat felt tight, but she refused to cry. Not in front of him, she wouldn't give him that. "Remember how I told you that with Henry the last bits of my faith and hope were gone?" When he didn't answer, she continued, "These weeks, I found it again. I had some faith—in us."

She smiled self-deprecatingly. "And, fool that am, I was ready to give my heart to the wrong man again."

She didn't give him time to respond. She said, "I hope you can finally leave the past in the past and move on at some point. I really do. Maybe when this house is nothing more than concrete ash…I don't know. But I'm done. I'm going home."

And with that, she turned around and went inside, to pack her things and to leave the red house and its sweet memories and unfulfilled wishes behind.

For good.

Thirteen

Christmas was supposed to be the happiest time of the year, and for most people it was. Presents and trees and Santa, happy couples and baby's first holiday bibs. How could anyone not smile at a neighbor and hum the chorus of "Jingle Bells." But for Tess, she just wanted to run out of NRR's office every day after work, get in her car and head home—hide under her bed until the whole holiday blew over.

It wasn't that she was a Scrooge or anything. She wanted to smile and sing, but it just wasn't in her.

Four days ago she'd left Tribute and the little red house and the man she had come to love once again. Today was Christmas Eve and that house had probably been bulldozed to the ground and that man was probably having a snowless holiday season in sunny California.

With a folder of new client information tucked under her arm, Tess walked by Mary's office.

When Mary spotted her, she called out, "Hey, Tess. Come here a sec."

Mary and Ethan had returned from their honeymoon a few days before, and Mary had been walking around the office like she was on cloud nine ever since.

Tess went in and sat across from her partner. There was a two-foot grinning Santa on the woman's desk, and Tess had to stop herself from knocking it to the ground. "What's up? I have someone waiting…"

"Oh, it won't take long." Mary flipped her blond hair over her shoulder and smiled. "I have something I want you to think about."

"Okay."

"You like kids, right?"

Tess laughed. "Of course I do. Mary what's this about?"

"I want you to be my baby's godmother."

A strange sadness moved over Tess. She was flattered, and incredibly honored by the offer—so pleased that Mary deemed her that close a friend. But right now the suggestion just served as a reminder of the family that she herself was never going to have.

She gave Mary her best smile. "Thank you for

thinking of me. It's an honor and a great responsibility. I need to think about it, okay?"

"Of course." Mary returned her smile. "After the holidays we'll talk."

Tess nodded. "After the holidays would be perfect."

She was just about to leave when Olivia walked in to Mary's office.

"Oh, good, Tess, just the person I wanted to see."

If Olivia was pregnant and wanting a godparent, too, Tess thought inanely, she was going to pretty much lose it right there.

But pregnancy was not what the pretty brunette wanted to see her about. "Your…client," she said with a half smile, "sent payment for service, but not a return address to send the receipt."

Tess asked, "Which client is that?"

"Mr. Sauer."

Her heart dropped. "He sent payment?"

"A rather large one."

Mary eyed her. "Have you upped your fee without telling us?"

"No." She turned to Olivia. "Listen, I don't want that money. Send it back."

"I can't."

"Then rip it up."

Mary came around her desk and touched her arm. "Tess, what's wrong. What's this about?"

"I knew he wasn't cool," Olivia said, staring at Tess's face. Then she looked at Mary and explained,

"Her client was also a past boyfriend, who obviously jerked her around."

Mary took Tess's hand but nodded at Olivia. "Rip up the check, Olivia."

"You bet," Olivia said quickly.

Tess looked up and gave her friend a thankful smile.

Olivia nodded. "Whatever you need, girl, okay?"

Tess took a deep breath. "Thanks, but I'm going to be fine." And she meant it. It might take a while to get there, maybe next month or next year, but she was going to be happy again.

"I'd better get going," she told the women. "I have a client waiting."

Mary squeezed her hand before releasing it. "Then go, we'll talk later."

Tess went into her office and sat at her desk. The man across from her was handsome, she noted. But in a boyish way. The man across from her had blue eyes, but there was no anger there, no arrogance there, no passion.

She was almost thankful for it.

She stuck out her hand. "Mr. Sumner, I'm Tess York. How can I help you today?"

The man looked grim and said, "I promised my mother I'd be married by New Year's Eve."

"And I take it you're not."

He shook his head. "Not yet."

"Do you have a girlfriend? Someone you're thinking about asking?"

He shook his head.

"And how would you like my help?

"Can you be my pretend fiancée?"

She smiled. "No, but I'll help you find the courage to tell your mother the truth."

He blanched. "How much is that going to cost me?"

Tess laughed, and it felt good. "Not a cent. This one's on the house."

He'd put it off another day. Soon they were going to give up on him and back out of the deal altogether.

Maybe that's what he wanted.

It was near midday, and Damien sat in front of the red house like a protester without a sign, staring at the bulldozers that were unmanned and stuck in the snow. They had been sitting there for days, and he had not allowed them to get any closer. He didn't know what was wrong with him. He should've been in California, back to work and on the road to recovery. Not sitting with his ass in the snow and his head on a cloud.

Damn Tess York. She'd ruined him again.

A car pulled into the icy driveway—a pickup truck, actually—and came to a skidding stop right in front of the walkway.

Damien had known it was only a matter of time before she would show up.

Dressed like Mrs. Claus, which she did every year for the kids who came into the store, Wanda got out of her truck and bellowed at him, "I don't have time for this, Damien. It's Christmas Eve."

"I know," Damien called dryly. "Shouldn't you be helping someone get dressed and on his sleigh right about now?"

Her eyes narrowed as she walked over to him and sat on the stoop. "Don't get smart with me, Damien Sauer."

"I'm sorry."

"Good. Now, what the hell are you doing?"

He shook his head. "Acting like an ass."

"I'll say. Four days of stopping that truck from doing its job…"

"Yeah…" He plowed his hands through his hair.

Her voice dropped, even softened a touch. "Do the deal, Damien."

"Can't."

"Why not?" she asked. "End it. Get it, and her, out of your system."

"The problem with that is I have a sneaking suspicion that taking down this house will not get her out of my system."

"What will, then?"

"I have no idea."

"It's freezing out here." She clicked her tongue. "This deal is sweet. It's a helluva lot of money—"

"I have enough money."

She snorted. "Please don't say, 'But I don't have her.'"

He threw her a sideways glance. "You are one sarcastic broad, Wanda."

"Damn right." She looked at him, studied him.

"Tell me you weren't foolish enough to fall in love with her again."

"I don't think I ever stopped loving her." It was the first time he'd admitted it, out loud and to himself, and it cut deeply.

Beside him, Wanda cursed like a race car driver.

"What are you going on about?" he asked her.

"I have to give you something," she said, thrusting a medium-size brown box at him. "Here."

"What's this?"

"Present."

"Wanda, you didn't have to—"

"I didn't. It's from the girl. Christmas present she ordered a few days ago at Remi's place." She frowned. "He asked me to get it to you."

Damien's heart twisted, and he felt like ramming his fist through a wall. After all they'd been through, after all he'd said, she'd gotten him a Christmas present.

He opened the package and his heart sank. It was a handmade snow globe with a model of the red house inside of it. Lights glowed from the inside and there was a Christmas tree and presents and two people by the fire.

He looked at the card. It read: "So you'll always know where you began, where you ended up and where you are always loved. Tess."

A muscle twitched in Damien's jaw, and he turned away.

"You could use it to knock out the window," Wanda said beside him. "Get the ball rolling.

Damien turned and stared at her. "What are you so angry about? Always expecting the worst, hoping for the worst. What is it? Did someone leave you heartbroken and pissed off, too?"

"Yes."

Her mouth was thin and hard, but her eyes held the sadness and pain of a lost love. Damien knew what she was feeling, and for the first time he saw what life, what his future, would be like if he remained as bitter as Wanda.

It wasn't a pretty picture.

He wanted what was in the snow globe.

He wanted her.

He dropped an arm around Wanda's shoulders. "What are we going to do, huh?"

"Not we." She faced him, lifted her chin and pretended her eyes didn't sparkle with tears. "I'm too old for forgiveness, but you're not."

He turned back and faced the bulldozers for the last time. "No. I'm not."

The word on the street was that Christmas day was to be spent with family. The women of No Ring Required might have started out as just partners, but in the past few months they had grown into so much more—friends. And if you asked any one of them, as they sat around the Christmas tree in the NRR office, family as well.

It was midmorning and all three women had left their homes, cats and sleeping fiancés, and had come to the office to eat Olivia's challah French toast and open their secret Santa gifts. A few days ago they had drawn names telling them which partner they would be picking out a present for.

Olivia had drawn Mary's name, and she went first. "Here you go, Mama."

Like an excited little kid, Mary took the small box and ripped it open. She squealed when she saw the pearl-and-diamond earrings inside.

"I love them, Liv," Mary said, giving her friend a huge grin. "Thank you."

"Pearl is the baby's birthstone," Olivia explained. "The diamonds are for you."

"As they should be." Mary laughed. "Thank you so much!"

"Okay. I drew your name, Olivia." Tess got up and pushed an enormous box toward the excited-looking brunette. "For you."

"Wow, thanks. Is someone going to pop out of here?"

"Yeah, Mac would just love that," Tess joked.

Grinning, Olivia tore at the Santa wrapping paper, then stopped and stared at what was inside—twelve bottles of what Olivia had always deemed the best Sicilian Olive Oil ever made. "Oh, my goodness, how did you find it?

As Olivia leaned over and hugged her, Tess said, "One of my clients this year is an Italian importer."

"I can't believe it," Olivia began, her eyes dancing with excitement. "A dozen bottles. Where to begin? Well, first thing I'm going to make will be Panzanella salad, then a basic tomato sauce, then of course—"

"Ease up there, Chef," Mary said on a laugh. "The culinary masterpieces can wait for five minutes. It's Tess's turn."

Olivia's cheeks turned pink. "Of course, sorry, Tess."

"No problem, Liv," Tess said with a smile as she took the box Mary held out in her direction. "We all know how deep your obsession runs."

"I hope I got the size right," Mary muttered.

The wrapping paper came off easily, and Tess knew right away that Mary had gotten her shoes. But when she opened the box and saw the rich red Jimmy Choo pumps she nearly fell over. They were beautiful. Something she'd never buy for herself, but always craved.

She looked up. "Thank you, Mary. They're stunning. And my size."

"They're supposed to be ruby slippers," Mary said with a little shrug. "My version."

"Like in the *Wizard of Oz?*" Olivia asked, confused.

Mary nodded, her eyes on Tess. "'No place like home,' you know? I just want you to always feel that way about this place and us. Whatever happened before, whoever came before, me, you and Olivia— we'll always be a family."

Heat shot into Tess's throat. She didn't want to get emotional in front of them, but it was too late. She swiped the tears from her eyes and shook her head. "Damn you both for making me cry," she said, laughing. "And thank you. Five years ago when I got into this business, I never would've thought I'd gain two best friends in the process."

Olivia grabbed her hand. "Me, neither."

"I say we make this a tradition," Mary said, her blue eyes brimming with emotion. "Every Christmas morning."

Tess nodded. "I second that suggestion."

"I'm in, too," Olivia said, picking up the torn wrapping paper to stick it in the trash. But as she passed by the tree, she paused. "Hey, there's something else here." She reached down and came up with a long envelope. "This has your name on it, Tess."

"Who's it from?" Tess looked at Mary.

She shook her head. "Not me."

Olivia shook her head, too. "Not me." She then looked down at the envelope again. "It says, 'Tess, keep the faith. Love, Santa.'" Olivia glanced up again. "What does that mean?"

A mixed bag of fear and warmth and wonder churned in Tess's belly. She knew exactly who the envelope was from. What she didn't know was what was inside and she was scared to find out. But both women were pushing her.

"Open it," Mary urged.

Olivia thrust the envelope into her hand. "Yeah, Tess. Come on."

Tess swallowed the hard lump in her throat and tore

open the envelope. There was a group of papers inside and she slipped them out, uncurled them and read the first page. Her pulse picked up speed and her head felt heavy, dizzy. It was the deed to the little red house. Damien had put it in her name. He had given it to her. He hadn't destroyed it.

"What is it?" Olivia asked softly.

I don't know, Tess thought wildly, tears building. What was it? An apology? Forgiveness? A final farewell. Tess looked up at them both and smiled. "I think it's a peace offering."

Olivia's brows lifted. "From a certain ex-client/ex-boyfriend?"

Tess nodded.

Mary looked from one to the other. "Okay, no more snippets of information. Someone better fill me in with the whole story."

Olivia laughed. "I will. But I think Tess has somewhere she needs to be right now."

With a quick smile at both of them, Tess grabbed her coat and purse and, as she was heading out the door, heard Olivia explain, "Remember that superhot guy with the blue eyes from your engagement party? Not that you should have, because you were only supposed to be looking at Ethan, but this man was hard to miss. Turns out he and Tess used to date…"

Traffic was light, just a few cars out on the road, heading for grandma's house or the airport or the 7-Eleven to pick up another carton of eggnog.

Tess made it to Tribute in two and a half hours. Her heart beat frantically as she got off the freeway and sped into town. But as she turned onto Main Street, then onto oh-so-familiar Yarr Lane, a sudden fear gripped her. What would she find when she got there? Would the house be just as she had left it, or had the bulldozers gotten to any of it? What about the inside?

And, God help her, what about Damien?

The answers to some of her questions came quickly as she pulled into the driveway and saw her sweet little cottage perfectly intact. There were even twinkle lights hanging from the rooflines and railings. The nerves in her belly eased, and she turned off the engine and got out of the car.

The wistful scent of turkey met her at the door. Not knowing what was inside, she decided to knock.

Damien opened the door, and his blue eyes glittered when he saw her. "Hey."

She nodded. "Hey."

"Welcome home."

His words, and the warm way he said them snaked through her. But she was too afraid to hope, to wonder what he was thinking and feeling.

She walked in, past him. He looked too good in jeans and a black sweater, his jaw clean shaven and his black hair thicker than usual.

"Merry Christmas," she said, noticing everything inside the house was just as she'd left it, and designed it—except for the blue spruce tree in the corner, heavily and oddly decorated with bubble lights, blue bulbs, paper ring ornaments and garland that was made out of pine cones and strawberries.

It was a mess, a homemade mess, but it made Tess smile. Clearly, Damien had done this.

She faced him. "I thought you'd be in California by now."

"And miss snow on Christmas? Not a chance. By the way, thank you for the snow globe. It was…perfect, exactly what I needed." He stared at her, his gaze heavy with longing. "You look good in this house."

She smiled tentatively. "So do you."

"You got the deed?"

"Yes." Her pulse jumped. She didn't want to ask, but she had to. "Was it another way of putting me and the past behind you?"

His eyes searched hers. "The past, yes. You, never." He reached for her hand, and when she gave it to him, he brought it to his mouth and kissed her palm. "I'm so sorry, Tess. I was such an idiot."

His touch made her weak, and all she could do was look at him, wait for him to say everything he needed to say.

"Fear makes people do crazy things," he said, lacing her fingers with his. "I thought I needed to hurt you to make myself hurt less. And that's just a load of bs— yet it's what I had to tell myself to stop myself from wanting you." His sincere gaze remained locked on her. "What I did was so wrong, Tess, and I almost lost you a second time because of it." A muscle twitched in his jaw and his voice dropped with emotion. "Tell me I have another chance to make it right."

His apology, his understanding of what had happened and why, stunned and amazed her. But she was still afraid to believe…. "Damien, I can never take back what I did—"

"Oh, sweetheart, I'm not asking you to. That's over, done. Doesn't matter. What matters is right now. What matters is that I love you."

She stared at him, her lips parted. "You love me?"

He nodded and pulled her into his arms. "Then, now and always." He kissed her neck, whispered in her ear, "Tell me you love me, too, before I go completely insane."

She smiled against his shoulder. "I love you, Damien. More than you'll ever know."

"I want to know." He pulled back so he could look at her. "Be my wife, Tess? Marry me and have my children. Let me give you the family you've always wanted."

Her heart soared with happiness. She couldn't believe what she was hearing. Never in a million years did she think this man would come to love her this much. She nodded, kept nodding.

"Is that a yes?" he said, laughing.

She stood on her tiptoes and kissed him squarely on the mouth. "That's a 'in a heartbeat.' That's a 'how about right now!'" She grinned. "Yes, Damien Sauer, I'll marry you."

He pulled her to him, his mouth covering hers

tenderly. When he eased back, he took her hand. "Come open your presents."

"I already have everything I could ever want. You and our little red house."

"Darling, there's so much more for you to enjoy." He led her over to the tree. "As you may have noticed, I'm not great with decorations. But there is one thing, right there in front of you that I am pretty proud of."

Tess looked at the branch sticking out in front of her, and her breath caught in her throat. Hanging on a thin length of pine was the most beautiful diamond ring she had ever seen.

Damien slipped it off the branch, then slipped it on her finger.

Tess stared at her hand. "It's so beautiful."

"You're so beautiful."

She looked up, felt as if she were floating on a cloud. She couldn't believe this day, this perfect Christmas day.

A holiday that had started off without a hope had turned into a season of true blessings.

Damien held her close as they stood by the tree. "Anything you want, it's yours."

"All I want is your love," she uttered with rich emotion.

"You have that, Tess."

And then he kissed her again. Not a soft sweet kiss this time, but a deep, heart-tugging, gut-clenching, knee-weakening full-mouth kiss.

"Damien," she uttered against his lips.

"Hmm?"

"You said I could have anything I want…."

He nuzzled her mouth, nipped at her lower lip. "Yes, my love. Of course. What is it?"

"That family you were talking about," she whispered.

"Yes?"

She grinned, brushed her lips teasingly against his. "Can we start making it right now?"

Damien slipped his hands beneath her and lifted her up. "Yes, my love," he said carrying her toward the bedroom. "Right now."

Epilogue

Dressed in a slightly over-the-top pink maternity bridesmaid gown, Mary glanced around the room. "Hearts, flowers and chocolate."

"Oh, my," Olivia finished, laughing.

The NRR threesome sat at one of the round reception tables, watching the wedding guests boogie on the white marble dance floor. The ballroom at Le Grande Hotel in downtown Minneapolis looked as though it had gone through a pink-and-red-and-white froufrou machine with all the ribbons, roses, hearts and toile. The wedding planner Tess hired had gone a little overboard with the *love* theme, but Tess didn't care. It was Valentine's Day. She had a beautiful white dress, great friends around her, a wonderful man who loved her and, for the first time in her life, a genuine enthusiasm about her future.

"This is one crazy wedding, Tess," Olivia remarked, pointing to the cupid ice sculpture.

"I think I like crazy," Tess said, grinning.

"You know you could've waited until the slow season, and Mary and I would have been happy to plan everything."

As the warm and familiar tune "We Are Family" blasted out of the speakers, Tess smiled widely at her girls. "Nope, I really couldn't wait."

"What do you mean?" Mary asked, confused.

Tess touched her stomach and shouted over the music. "Bun in the oven. I mean, a little Sauer in the oven."

Olivia squealed and hugged Tess. Mary smiled and shook her head. "Sorry, I'm just too big and uncomfortable to lean over."

"You're only six months pregnant, Mary," Olivia said, laughing.

Mary glared at her. "Just wait."

Olivia grinned, her brown eyes sparkling. "We are waiting. For a little while, anyway. I want my man all to myself."

"I hear that." Tess laughed. "Speaking of your man…and ours, too…"

"What?" Olivia said, her dark brows drawing together.

"Here they come."

All three women turned. Walking across the dance

floor toward them, looking tall, handsome and oh so wicked in the strange light cast by the red and pink decorations, were Ethan, Mac and Damien.

Mary gave a low wolf whistle.

Olivia muttered a dry, "Wow."

"Did we land some seriously good-looking man flesh or what?" Mary remarked dryly. "How lucky are we?"

"Very." Tess laughed. "But then again, they got pretty lucky, too."

The three women turned back to each other and smiled, They understood now that, through this newly found friendship and the stories of the past that they had shared with each other, they were forever linked. They had an unspoken promise. They were family, partners and there for each another always.

For Tess, it was not just a happy wedding day, it was a hopeful one—for all of them.

The future looked very bright indeed.

* * * * *

*Turn the page for a sneak preview
of the first book in the new miniseries*
DIAMONDS DOWN UNDER
from Silhouette Desire®
VOWS & A VENGEFUL GROOM
by Bronwyn Jameson

*Available January 2008
(SD #1843)*

*Silhouette Desire®
Always Powerful, Passionate and Provocative*

Kimberley Blackstone didn't notice the waiting horde of media until it was too late. Flashbulbs exploded around her like a New Year's light show. She skidded to a halt, so abruptly her trailing suitcase all but overtook her.

This had to be a case of mistaken identity. Surely. Kimberley hadn't been on the paparazzi hit list for close to a decade, not since she'd estranged herself from her billionaire father and his headline-hungry diamond business.

But no, it was *her* name they called. *Her* face was the focus of a swarm of lenses that circled her like avid hornets. Her heart started to pound with fear-fueled adrenaline.

What did they want?

What was going on?

With a rising sense of bewilderment she scanned the crowd for a clue, and her gaze fastened on a tall, leonine figure forcing his way to the front. A tall, familiar figure. Her head came up in stunned recognition, and their gazes collided across the sea of heads before the cameras erupted with another barrage of flashes, this time right in her exposed face.

Blinded by the flashbulbs—and by the shock of that momentary eye-meet—Kimberley didn't realize his intent until he'd forged his way to her side, possibly by the sheer strength of his personality. She felt his arm wrap around her shoulder, pulling her into the protective shelter of his body, allowing her no time to object. No chance to lift her hands to ward him off.

In the space of a hastily drawn breath, she found herself plastered knee-to-nose against six feet two inches of hard-bodied male.

Ric Perrini.

Her lover for ten torrid weeks, her husband for ten tumultuous days.

Her ex for ten tranquil years.

After all this time, he should not have felt so familiar but, oh dear, he did. She knew the scent of that body and its lean, muscular strength. She knew its heat and its slick power and every response it could draw from hers.

She also recognized the ease with which he'd taken control of the moment and the decisiveness of his deep voice when it rumbled close to her ear. "I have a car waiting outside. Is this your only luggage?"

Kimberley nodded. "I assume you will tell me," she said tightly, "what this welcome party is all about."

"Not while the welcome party is within earshot. No."

Barking a request for the cameramen to stand aside, Perrini took her hand and pulled her into step with his ground-eating stride. Kimberley let him, because he was right, damn his arrogant, Italian-suited hide. Despite the speed with which he whisked her across the airport terminal, she could almost feel the hot breath of the pursuing media on her back.

This was neither the time nor the place for explanations. Inside his car, however, she would get answers.

Now that the initial shock had been blown away—by the haste of their retreat, by the heat of her gathering indignation, by the rush of adrenaline fired by Perrini's presence and the looming verbal battle—her brain was starting to tick over. This had to be her father's doing. And if it was a Howard Blackstone publicity ploy, then it had to be about Blackstone Diamonds, the company that ruled his life.

The knowledge made her chest tighten with a familiar ache of disillusionment.

She'd known her father would be flying in from Sydney for today's opening of the newest in his chain of exclusive, high-end jewelry boutiques. The opulent shop front sat adjacent to the rival business where Kimberley worked. No coincidence, she thought bitterly, just as it was no coincidence that Ric Perrini was here in Auckland ushering her to his car.

Perrini was Howard Blackstone's right-hand man, second in command at Blackstone Diamonds, a legacy of his short-lived marriage to the boss's daughter. No doubt her father had sent him to fetch her; the question was *why?*

* * * * *

Get swept away down under with the glitz and glamour of the Blackstone empire as Kimberley tries to determine the real reason behind her "reunion" with Ric....

Look for
VOWS & A VENGEFUL GROOM
by Bronwyn Jameson
In stores January 2008

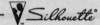

INTRIGUE

INTRIGUE'S ULTIMATE HEROES

6 heroes. 6 stories.
One month to read them all.

For one special month, Harlequin Intrigue
is dedicated to those heroes among men.
Desirable doctors, sexy soldiers, brave
bodyguards—they are all
Intrigue's Ultimate Heroes.

In January, collect all 6.

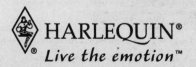

HARLEQUIN®
Live the emotion™

REQUEST YOUR FREE BOOKS

2 FREE NOVELS
PLUS 2
FREE GIFTS!

Silhouette®

Desire

Passionate, Powerful, Provocative!

YES! Please send me 2 FREE Silhouette Desire® novels and my 2 FREE gifts. After receiving them, if I don't wish to receive any more books, I can return the shipping statement marked "cancel." If I don't cancel, I will receive 6 brand-new novels every month and be billed just $3.80 per book in the U.S., or $4.47 per book in Canada, plus 25¢ shipping and handling per book and applicable taxes, if any*. That's a savings of almost 15% off the cover price! I understand that accepting the 2 free books and gifts places me under no obligation to buy anything. I can always return a shipment and cancel at any time. Even if I never buy another book from Silhouette, the two free books and gifts are mine to keep forever.

225 SDN EEXJ   326 SDN EEXL

Name	(PLEASE PRINT)

Address	Apt.

City	State/Prov.	Zip/Postal Code

Signature (if under 18, a parent or guardian must sign)

Mail to the **Silhouette Reader Service™**:
IN U.S.A.: P.O. Box 1867, Buffalo, NY 14240-1867
IN CANADA: P.O. Box 609, Fort Erie, Ontario L2A 5X3

Not valid to current Silhouette Desire subscribers.

Want to try two free books from another line?
Call 1-800-873-8635 or visit www.morefreebooks.com.

* Terms and prices subject to change without notice. NY residents add applicable sales tax. Canadian residents will be charged applicable provincial taxes and GST. This offer is limited to one order per household. All orders subject to approval. Credit or debit balances in a customer's account(s) may be offset by any other outstanding balance owed by or to the customer. Please allow 4 to 6 weeks for delivery.

Your Privacy: Silhouette is committed to protecting your privacy. Our Privacy Policy is available online at www.eHarlequin.com or upon request from the Reader Service. From time to time we make our lists of customers available to reputable firms who may have a product or service of interest to you. If you would prefer we not share your name and address, please check here. ☐

SDE

Silhouette®

nocturne™

Jachin Black always knew he was an outcast.
Not only was he a vampire, he was a vampire
banished from the Sanguinas society. Jachin, forced
to survive among mortals, is determined to buy
his way back into the clan one day.

Ariel Swanson, debut author of a vampire novel, could
be the ticket he needs to get revenge and take his
rightful place among the Sanguinas again. However,
the unsuspecting mortal woman has no idea of the
dark and sensual path she will be forced to travel.

Look for

RESURRECTION: THE BEGINNING

by

PATRICE MICHELLE

Available January 2008 wherever you buy books.

Silhouette® Desire

COMING NEXT MONTH

SDCNM1